CW01023864

PARTUM

A Novella

PARTUM

A Novella

EV KNIGHT

PARTUM

A Novella

Published by Sinister Smile Press
P.O. Box 637
Newberg, OR 97132

Trade Paperback ISBN – 978-1-953112-19-4

www.sinistersmilepress.com

DEDICATION

To Stephanie and Isabelle, who understand.

CHAPTER 1

I DON'T HEAR THE keys in the lock or the door opening. The conversation in the chatroom is intense—a new member has shared his ordeal, and he mentioned the smell of ammonia. I'm following the discussion intently.

I've added my input just as CJ yells, "Crazy piece of shit fuckin' bit me. Goddamn it!"

I jump and squeal. He should not be home at three-thirty in the afternoon. If he sees what I've been doing, he'll be upset. No time to shut it down, so I divert by hurrying to meet him in the foyer. I feel like a teenager caught watching porn.

"What happened?" I rub my hands on my three-day-old jeans and meet up with him in the kitchen. He beelines to the sink. Cold water runs magenta beneath a gash on his left wrist. CJ grits his teeth and breathes deeply through them.

"Third one this week. I don't know what kind of fucking drugs they're doing these days, but..." He pauses to flex his fingers and make a fist. "Can you just stitch this up, or whatever?"

I take his hand and do a quick examination. Whatever bit him tore back a piece of skin leaving a semi-circular flap around the deepest part of the wound.

"I think you should go to the ER. You need some antibiotics and—"

"Just stitch it up, Lena. Please. I don't have time to spend all day in the ER. I got some antibiotics left over from the last time I got bit. I'll take them."

Only the bite on his wrist is not like any of the other bites he's had. As a police officer, CJ's been hit, kicked, spat on, clawed, and bitten more times than I can count, but I've never seen a human bite as vicious looking as this one. There is no arguing with him, though. Not now, anyway. Not when he already worries that his wife lost her mind almost a year ago.

"Here." I press a wet, and folded, paper towel hard against the wound. "Hold this tight. I'll go get my stuff."

I hope he'll sit and wait, but CJ is a pacer, always moving. If he walks around the corner and sees the computer screen, I'll never hear the end of it, and I can tell he's in no mood to be reasoned with.

The bin—filled with unused, or expired, surgical supplies I'd quietly adopted from the OR back when I was working—waits patiently in the laundry room cupboard. Rather than spend time digging out everything I might need, I carry the whole thing out to the table. CJ is not in the kitchen, though. My heart trips over itself and then tries to scuttle backwards into my throat. His heavy breathing leads me to him, although I already know where he is.

My handle—BridgeMom—stands out bold on the screen, basically screaming to CJ to *look what she wrote this time!* He's bent over the desk, scrolling through the previous comments. I clear my throat. Fury flashes across his face, but exasperation and pity make a home there.

"Can you just come sit down at the table and not say anything?" I plead. We've been through the fights, the accusations, the grief. I don't have the strength to do it again.

"You have an appointment with Dr. Preston today?"

"At four-thirty." He nods and lets it go, but he shuts down the website before following me back to the table.

I lay a once-sterile blue drape over the dark cherry table-top, and he rests his arm on it. We settle into silence as I clean the bite, draw up about four milliliters of lidocaine, change needles to a smaller gauge, and begin injecting. CJ utters a stream of profanities and stomps his foot on the slate floor. Funny how we had to buy a new round top table so Bridget wouldn't hit her head into a corner when learning to walk, yet the cold, unforgiving tile stayed. New parents are never truly prepared for reality.

"Does the doc know about your newest obsession? I mean, have you asked her about those studies on SIDS?" he asks. I appreciate the conversational manner he's using since I know, inside, he is seething.

I promised him I wouldn't log onto any more 'aliens among us' sites, as he calls them. Yet…

"She's a therapist, not a medical doctor. What would she know about SIDS?" I start to suture, and CJ's muscles relax as soon as I place the first stitch. The lidocaine is working, even if it is expired. I decide to change the subject. "So, what did this guy do? The one you arrested who bit you?"

CJ studies my face. Probably deciding whether to let the therapy question slide, or maybe debating if I can handle the information about his strange arrest. Finally, he sighs.

"First of all, it wasn't a guy. It was a woman. And she didn't really *do* anything. One minute, she was pushing a shopping cart in the produce section and the next, she went wild. Growling and lunging at customers. I mean, for a good ten minutes, she was aggressively insane. I was out at the pumps and got the call, so I ran over and tried to subdue her. I had one cuff on her when she bit me. I maced her. I tased her. And, Lena, nothing stopped her. I managed to back her up to a support pole and cuff her to it."

My hands are shaking, so I stop suturing. "What was wrong with her?"

CJ shrugs. "Dunno. By the time the paramedics got there, she was back to normal. Crying, scared, asking what happened."

"But you said she was the third one this week?"

"Has to be drug related. Some kind of drug seizure

or withdrawal, or something. I wasn't there for the other two, but Paul and Kelley were. Described the same thing. I thought they were exaggerating, but now I've seen it for myself."

I nod, thinking.

"Hey," CJ play-slaps my cheek with his good hand. "Don't get any ideas about this, okay? There is nothing paranormal, or extraterrestrial, going on here. I don't want you trying to rationalize it to fit with your conspiracy theories."

I love CJ, I do, but, sometimes, I want to just split his head open when he starts with the condescending attitude and refusal to even consider the possibilities of alien life and its interaction with humans.

I smile and force a laugh. "I'm not crazy, CJ. Maybe you are, though, for not going to the ER to have a doctor stitch you up."

"Why would I do that when I have my own personal surgical tech?"

"I'm not a tech anymore," I say and finish the stitches. He doesn't take the bait.

"Looks good to me," he announces, looking at his bandaged hand.

"Take your antibiotic."

"Yeah, yeah." He grabs the bottle out of the cupboard, along with a snack-sized bag of BBQ chips. "And don't you forget to tell Dr. Preston about the SIDS stuff."

I wave him off and stand motionless with my hands on my hips. I wait to hear the car start up. I have every intention to go back to that chatroom. The door swings open, and CJ's head pops back into the house.

"Stay off that website, Lena. You promised." He pulls the door shut. I hear the car reversing down the drive.

He's gone. I'm alone.

A lump fills my throat, and my facial muscles contort to release the tears. It happens like this sometimes. *Grief.*

My knees buckle, bringing me to the ground, where I curl up like a baby. I hold myself, and I cry.

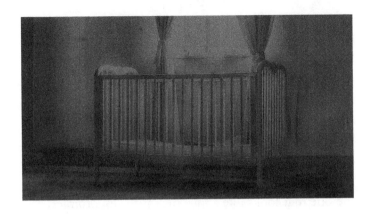

CHAPTER 2

D R. PRESTON'S OFFICE is in the basement of her home. Descending the concrete steps to the locked door always feels like descending into Hell to be judged for all my sins. I press the buzzer and wonder why she never seems to have another client. At least, I've never seen one. The door clicks, and I enter the familiar, yet unwelcoming, space I've come to loathe.

"Hi, Lena. Come on in. Let me just grab my notes, and we'll get started. Can I get you anything? Water? Tea?"

I want tea, but shake my head. "No, thank you."

I take off my shoes, jacket, and drop my purse beside the coatrack before entering the carpeted consultation room. The only light comes from two windows, near the ceiling behind her desk, and a large, floor model salt lamp that sits in a corner created between the couch and a big, overstuffed chair. Dr. Preston always sits in a sturdy wooden armchair, upholstered in red and gold brocade, with a small side table that swings in front of her. She puts her tea and folder on it but never seems to take any notes.

I pass the bookcase lining the walls. There are no books on the shelves, though, just antique medical equipment—instruments from old asylums that look more like torture devices than professional tools. I know the one that looks like an ice pick is for lobotomies, but the one that looks like a tiny ice auger makes me shiver. I shuffle past the case of medieval punishments and choose the couch, because that was the seat I took at my first appointment. Although I really want to sit in the comfy chair, I feel as if I should stick with the choice I made before. There are throw pillows, and an afghan, on both the couch and chair, and an electric fireplace, which I think is to make you feel comfortable, like a guest.

But the art gives away the ruse. All the art in the room is abstract. Meant to make you think, meant to draw your eye, and begin to question what it means to you. Dr. Preston never gives you the answers. It's a test.

I never pay much attention to the ombre painting in autumn hues or the one with all the circles and spots. It's the bone-white sculpture on the mantle that distracts me. Is it bone? The curves and twists of various widths make me think no, but that might mean it's not bone *of this earth*. There are very tiny bones in the inner ear with the strangest curves and shapes, so who's to say? I wonder if Dr. Preston only puts that piece out when I am coming, as if she knows, or, maybe she is sending me the message that she *does know.*

Dr. Preston sits down and opens my folder. "What's on your mind today, Lena? You seem pensive." She stirs her tea but does not take her eyes off me.

I could ask her what the sculpture is made of, but I don't, because I know she wants me to. Instead, I shrug. "Same old, I guess."

"I was hoping today, we could go back to the time just after Bridget was born. I know we talked a little about that when you first came in, but I'd like to go back and talk about your depression at that time." She sips her tea. I wonder if it is herbal or decaffeinated—she is so calm.

"Lots of women get postpartum depression. It's very common," I reply. *What does it matter now? Bridget is dead.*

"Yes, you're right, and there is nothing to be ashamed of. It's so hard to be a first-time mom. Heck, I guess it's hard every time." She laughs but there's no smile in it.

"Bridget was born five weeks early and that made her colicky, I never slept."

"You'd mentioned that. Did CJ help you at all? I mean, during the nights, at least."

"No. CJ was on night shifts. He didn't take time off, because he wanted to save his vacation days for summer when Bridget wasn't so fragile. We were going to fly to California to visit his parents."

"Surely he had days off?"

He did, didn't he? I must have slept at some point.

9

I just don't really remember. Those days blurred together. I say nothing, shrugging.

"How long did she suffer with colic?"

"Months. At least two, maybe three. We'd just got into a better sleeping routine when she…" I don't finish. Dr. Preston already knows.

"I can't imagine the stress of all those sleepless nights, alone, with a baby that wouldn't stop crying, in addition to all the hormonal changes associated with the postpartum period."

I look up at her, searching her eyes, her face, for a tell that says she is insinuating that I killed my baby. Wouldn't she be something, then? **Local Therapist Cracks Mysterious Death of Four-Month-Old: The Mommy Did It!**

"Bridget died of SIDS," I remind her. "There was an autopsy."

"Yes, I know. I'm thinking about all the stress you had before her death, and then having to deal with her loss, too. You're doing very well, you know? Some women wouldn't be able to function after everything you've gone through this past year."

"Thank you." I relax and wonder what she would do if I got up and moved to the comfy chair. I don't.

"Did your doctor start you on any antidepressants? I know you said you'd never been to counseling, but surely she gave you something to help."

"She did, but I didn't take it. I was afraid it might make me fall asleep and not hear her crying. I was all by myself at night."

"I see. So, you suffered through three months of colic? Tough woman."

I wonder—if a gust of wind blew through the sculpture, would it make a noise? I imagine a humming sound, probably. Low, like white noise from those machines that help you sleep. I must have slept some in those first few months. Even nights alone, there had to be some intervals of silence.

Dr. Preston watches me watch the sculpture again. I don't want to talk about that time. I don't want to remember how hard it was to love my baby then. I don't want to tell her how I sometimes turned the video monitor off and shut the door, telling myself that many people recommend letting the baby learn to soothe herself. I don't want to think about how maybe the night she died wasn't the first night *they* took her.

I sit up and refocus. "Yes. But we made it, and things got better…for a while."

"Tell me, Lena, did you ever have scary thoughts, or nightmares, about harm coming to you or the baby? I'm not accusing you of anything, mind you. I ask because it is not uncommon for intrusive thoughts to invade our minds under a great deal of stress."

I decide it is time to address the elephant in the room. "Did CJ call you?"

Her mouth drops open. She holds her teacup two inches from her face, frozen, but for only a second, then she sips. She says nothing after that, for longer than a second. Maybe as long as a minute.

"Yes."

"He wanted us to talk about the study I found. It's about SIDS and elevated ammonia levels found during autopsy."

"Yes, he mentioned that, but I'm not sure it's something we should get into."

"Why? Isn't that why I'm here? It's not because Bridget had colic, or because I had postpartum depression. She got better, and I got better, and then she disappeared for, what seemed like, only minutes and when she came back, she died. Maybe they brought her back dead? I mean, we didn't touch her then, only looked to see that she was back in her crib. But *CJ* asked *me*. He noticed the strong smell. He asked me if I had been cleaning her room that day. This isn't me making up false memories. So, this study, and the fact that many people who have been abducted by aliens talk about the smell of ammonia—that's what I'm doing here today. I'm here because you, and CJ, and probably most of the world, think I'm crazy. You all think my postpartum depression, followed by Bridget's death, set me up to lose my mind. So, why not talk about it, Dr. Preston? Why not get to the meat of it?"

She draws a long, deep breath and picks up her empty teacup. She closes my folder and stands. She says nothing. It's her way of letting me calm down. I know the trick. I may as well pretend I'm improving. I don't know why I try to change her mind.

I keep my eyes forward, rest my chin on my hands, and my elbows on my knees. I hear her go to the tea cart and set the cup down, and then wait for her to enter my peripheral vision, as she goes to her desk to leave my chart. Finally, she turns and leans against the solid wood monstrosity she uses to remind her "clients" that she is still the one in charge.

"Lena, I'm going to be honest with you. I am not familiar with the theories on SIDS, I haven't read this study you mentioned, nor am I any kind of specialist on alien abduction psychology. Therefore, I don't feel qualified to discuss those possibilities with you. If you don't want to try remembering or revisiting, at least, the unfortunately short period of time Bridget was alive, then I am not sure we can move forward today."

I say nothing nor do I look up at her. But, still, I can see that she has picked something up and writes on it.

"Before our next session, I would like you to take this to your family doctor and ask her to consider this medication for you. Also, I would like you to seriously consider taking it. I think it will help you move forward."

I take the note, fold it, and put it in my pocket. "Sure," I say. But I won't. I stand up, too. "I guess I'll call you after that to make an appointment?"

She nods. "If I don't hear back from you in two weeks, I'd like to call and check in. Is that okay?"

"Sure," I say. "Thanks."

I let myself out.

On the drive home I think about what Dr. Preston said about not being a specialist in alien abductions. *Of course!* That's the problem. I need to find a therapist who specializes in treating patients who have dealt with

extraterrestrial trauma. I check the clock on the dash—
five-fifteen. I have a little over two hours before CJ gets
home.

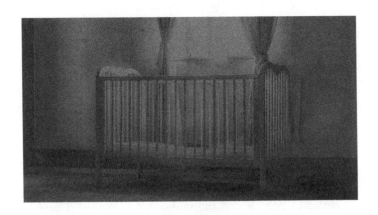

CHAPTER 3

T HE *SURVIVORS OF* Encounters of the *Fourth Kind* (*SEFK*) group I follow is holding a conference in Massachusetts in two weeks. A psychologist attending specializes in alien abductions and hypnosis. Until today, I hadn't considered signing up, although many of the folks I talk to daily are going and have encouraged me to go. What excuse can I use with CJ? I decide to register, pay the reservation fees, and worry about asking for forgiveness later, rather than asking permission.

My 'new email' notification pings, so I open it, assuming it's the confirmation. It's not. Not really. It's a notice from the group. It seems that Amherst, Massachusetts, where the conference is being held, has had a recent outbreak of "violent activity." While they are proceeding with the conference, they recommend we do not venture out by ourselves at any time. I read and re-read it, thinking about what CJ said about these strange seizures people are having. Could it be related? Springfield, Ohio, is a long way from Amherst.

"Now you're buying in to conspiracy theories," I tell myself. Talking out loud to myself, I've decided, is less madness and more like diversion therapy. If I have to sit in this silent house every day, without any human interaction, I really will lose it. Eventually, I'd like to go back to work, be productive, help take care of people. But, for now, I'm still grieving. I'm still suffering. I need closure—but first, I need to go to the conference.

Back in the chatroom, everyone is discussing the email. Of course, on a website like this, there will be some crazies—nut jobs who swear the government is allowing aliens to do research on its citizens.

MIBA51: heard about cases like this in other areas. clusters of em—could be implants for brain control or GPS tracking. might be causing seizures.

RubyJ1976: i belong to a few sites like this. haven't heard anyone claiming to be an abductee having these seizures tho.

DrBKyVa: Seems like a virus or spirochete—rabies or tertiary syphilis. I don't think we need to get carried away. Not really in our field of study.

MIBA51: that's what they want u 2 think...

TomSmith: I think we should all stay alert, keep an eye on these cases, gather as much factual evidence as we can. We'll add a post-conference discussion one night. Everyone still going?

BridgeMom: I just signed up. DH will kill me...trying to think of an excuse to feed him.

AlienAlli: @BridgeMom you had the baby that died, right? if u fly into Boston, there is a big medical conference going on here that week on Postpartum Depression and Psychosis get some info on it and tell him ur going there.

RubyJ1976: what if it's an alien parasite? Like that puppet masters movie? the one with donald sutherland?

BridgeMom: that's perfect AA! ty. also, DH is a cop. says there have been 3 cases in a week here of these weird seizure things. a lady actually bit him. I'll try to get more info from him.

TomSmith: @BridgeMom, I'm flying into Boston too. Maybe we can share a rental?

MIBA51: we need to find a doctor who has treated some of these seizure victims & see if they checked ammonia levels.

"Shit." I forgot to check the mail on my way back from Dr. Preston's. Bridget's medical records should be here today. I check the clock. There's time. I exit the chat and close the computer.

The box is empty. I stare into the void. *Is it a holiday?* It isn't. I know. It's a rare day to get no mail. Hell, we're still getting parenting magazines and formula coupons almost six months after Bridget's death. My stomach sends up a distress signal filled with acid. I swallow it down. CJ came home early. If there was other mail but not the big envelope filled with copies of labs and doctors' notes, I'd feel a little less stressed. But no mail means CJ probably grabbed it on his way out. All I can do now is pray he just tucked it up under his visor, where he keeps his paperwork, and hasn't yet gone through it.

Dinner is waiting for him—a quick stir fry—when he walks through the door. I see the pack of mail in hand. The large, white envelope almost glows like a beacon amongst the other bills and junk loan offers. Pretending not to notice it, I plate our food and set it on the table. He never changes out of his uniform, or showers, before dinner. I always did, but I was in the operating room all day, so it seemed like the right thing to do. CJ doesn't think the same way.

"How was the rest of your day?" he asks.

I shrug. "Fine."

"How'd it go with Dr. Preston?"

"The same. She didn't want to talk about the articles. She said she is not a specialist on that sort of thing, so she didn't think it would be helpful. All she wanted to ask about was my depression and Bridget's colic."

CJ stands up and does a slow lap around the kitchen island. I watch him but say nothing. He is thinking. Sometimes, when we fight, he does this to calm down. I don't think we are fighting. His plate is empty, and I am not hungry anymore. I take our plates to the sink. His pacing takes him to the far side of the island. I pretend his behavior is not, in the least, abnormal and walk to the living room. We have subscriptions to multiple streaming services, yet, there never seems to be anything to watch. As I mindlessly scroll past all the movies and recommendations, he enters the room from the far side of the kitchen. He is behind the sofa where I sit.

Chills roll up the back of my neck, and I wonder if he can see them. I'm clenching my jaw, waiting for whatever CJ has to say. When he finally walks around the couch and stands in front of me, I see he holds the envelope. It's been opened, and the stack of papers are pulled out, held in CJ's unwounded right hand.

"I read through these at work. My God, Lena. I had no idea." The volume of his voice is low, his pace steady, but his tone waivers.

I don't know if he is waiting for me to say something. I decide to let him deflate fully before I speak, so, I try to keep eye contact, but say nothing.

"Fifteen!" Now he yells. He slaps the papers with his wounded hand, and I see him flinch, for just a second, before his face turns red, and his muscles clench. "Fifteen visits in her four short months. Visits, Lena, not phone calls. They don't send copies of that, but they're mentioned in the notes."

He's angry because I took her to the doctor? "CJ— she had so many things. Marks, bruises. I thought maybe there was something else wrong. Maybe they were signs of some disease causing her colic." His nostrils flare and he almost snorts, like a mad horse. "I wanted her to get better," I add, to be clear.

CJ throws the papers at me. They spread out in the air, and some fall to the floor, before the bulk hits the couch beside me and slides. In slow motion, it would have been beautiful—like doves taking flight at a wedding. Instead, it's just an unimpressive magic trick that turned a neat, organized documentary of suffering into a depiction of the chaos left behind. I pick them up. I don't like it, the disregard for anything that carries Bridget's name.

"Do you know what Munchausen by Proxy is?" CJ asks.

"Yes, CJ, of course I do."

"So, you understand why that diagnosis might show up in her records? They thought you were crazy! They thought you were hurting Bridget on purpose!"

I hold my hands over my ears. He is just trying to hurt me. He misses Bridget, too. Sometimes, I wonder if he blames himself. Sometimes, I wonder if I blame him for her death. Maybe she could have been saved. He deflects a lot. If he makes me believe I was crazy, or that I lost my mind, then he can blame me. I'm not going to look at the papers he's tossed, because doing so would just give validation to his accusations. But to me, it proves that there *were* marks on Bridget. She really did have documented medical issues.

Signs she'd been abducted more than once.

"Lena!" CJ pulls my hands away, and I blink.

"What? What do you want me to say?"

"There was one visit for some kind of weird rash on her thigh. The doctor wrote a note saying it was in a precise, organized pattern that was similar to that of a meat mallet! A Goddamned meat mallet, Lena! What did you do to her?"

PARTUM

My heart stops. I remember that. I was changing her diaper first thing in the morning, and I saw them—perfectly spaced small red marks. She cried when I ran my finger over them. But, I would never...

"I would never hurt her, CJ. You know that. You know me. Come on! I loved Bridget." I'm sobbing now. Why did he have to do this? "Why am I still here and not at work? Why am I the one going to counseling? Because *I* was here with her twenty-four/seven. Me. Not you. I had a bond that you'll never understand. I carried her, I laid strapped to a table while they cut her out of me, and I was with her until she died. If I'm crazy, it's with grief. It's insanity trying to understand what happened to my baby girl." I can't say anymore. Sadness wraps itself around me like a weighted blanket, and I give in.

It's dark in the house when I feel CJ's hand on my thigh. I fell asleep on the couch. CJ has cleaned up the papers and covered me with a blanket.

"It's eleven. You should come to bed," he says.

CHAPTER 4

THE NIGHT BRIDGET died was the first time CJ and I had sex since before she was born. It was also the last night we had sex. Bridget's colic, and my postpartum depression, would not allow for any sort of a libido. But at four-months-old, she settled down and began sleeping better.

I was so tired; I thought I would be able to quickly catch up on sleep, but it was the opposite. With Bridget sleeping longer, I became more paranoid. Was she okay? What if she stopped breathing? CJ bought a video monitor and put it on my nightstand. I suppose he thought I would rest better knowing I could check on her anytime I opened my eyes. Instead, I lay awake every night just staring at the screen, watching the rise and fall of her little chest.

CJ tried a few times, leading up to that night, to initiate sex, but with my attention fixated on the monitor, it never went anywhere. Once, we'd made it as far as CJ crawling on top of me before I turned to check the screen. He got so angry with me, he swiped it off the nightstand and across the room. It unplugged easily, under his force, and went blank. I lost my mind. It was as if he had hit our baby and not some electronic equipment. I was in a frenzy. I slapped him, I screamed. I grabbed up the monitor and took it to the living room, where I planned to spend the rest of the night, and who knows how much longer after that. The noise woke Bridget up, though, and I spent the night holding her on the rocking chair in her room.

The next day, I discovered that CJ had put the monitor back in our room, plugged in and turned on, before he'd left for work. He never spoke of it again and didn't try to initiate anything again until *that* night. Even then, it wasn't really CJ pushing. I'd just been to the gynecologist for my annual exam, and she asked how my sex life was going since the new baby. I told her everything, broke down in her office. I told her about Bridget's health issues and my lack of sleep, and how even though things were much better, I was still a paranoid mess. She calmly explained that this was quite normal for someone in my position, but that, sometimes, these kinds of stressors, can destroy an otherwise healthy relationship. She said she'd seen a lot of divorces occur after the birth of a special-needs child, or even after a stressful postpartum period. She recommended we plan a date night and schedule sex.

I didn't want to lose CJ. I loved him, and I knew

some of this was my fault. So, I went home with a goal. I was going to have sex with my husband. I made a nice dinner, we had some wine, and I put Bridget to bed at eight-thirty. CJ and I took our wine and glasses to the bedroom where we put on some R&B—but not too loud—and we snuggled. When things started getting more intense, I told myself not to look at the monitor.

At some point, I couldn't help it. I did. I turned my head just enough to glance at the screen—quickly—before he could notice. I swear I saw an empty crib. *No Bridget.* My heart stumbled, and I caught my breath. I wanted to push CJ off me and go see my baby, but the rational side of my brain said I was being fooled. Of course, Bridget was in her crib. Where else would she be? Meanwhile, CJ had taken my change as a sign that I was nearing climax, so he worked harder. I shut my eyes tight and tried to focus. *Bridget is fine, Bridget is fine, Bridget is fine.* The mantra looped in my head in rhythm with CJ's thrusts. I felt his torso stiffen, all the muscles tensing. I knew he was close, that he wouldn't notice if I took another look just to assure myself that Bridget was in bed, asleep, and well.

The image on the screen was an empty crib. No Bridget, no blanket. Something was very wrong. CJ grunted and slammed against me. I tried to remain calm until he slid his sweaty body off me. He padded to the bathroom to wash up.

"I'm going to go peek in on the baby," I called and threw on my robe.

There must have been a full moon that night,

because I remember how her room radiated with a blue glow. I could easily see without turning on the light. I kept her blinds up all the time, because I thought it would help her to learn to nap during the day. I don't know why; I had a lot of crazy thoughts like that when she was alive.

In the fairytale darkness, I could see that her crib was indeed empty. I couldn't process what I saw because it made no sense. I'd only put her to bed a little over an hour before. Her windows were locked. She was only four months old. She did not crawl out of the crib. Even so, I rushed around the room looking behind, and under, everything. I opened the closet. Nothing. I stood in the center of the room hyperventilating. A warm, glop of semen slid out of me and ran down my leg, reminding me of what a terrible mother I was.

"CJ!" I didn't wait for an answer. I ran back to our bedroom. He'd already curled up under the blankets and was sleeping. He probably hadn't even glanced at the monitor. I shook him by the shoulder.

"What the...? What?" he said when he saw my face.

"Bridget's gone. She's missing, I mean. Please, CJ, get up. She's not in her crib!" I'm not sure exactly what I said, but it got him up—with a scowl on his face. He didn't believe me. I couldn't go back in there and face the truth, but I couldn't be alone in our room, either. I followed behind CJ but stopped at the threshold of Bridget's door. I watched him walk in and stare into the crib. I waited for his panicked look.

He turned around and frowned at me. "She's right

there, sleeping," he whispered.

"What?" I said, and he shushed me.

"Look for yourself." He pointed to the crib.

God help me, I didn't go back in. I couldn't. I was so afraid—partly to see that she was there, which meant I might, indeed, be crazy, but also because I knew what I saw, and her room frightened me.

"Come on, silly," he said shaking his head. "Let's go back to bed. Enjoy the sleep."

Back in our room, on the monitor, Bridget slept. I rolled away from the image and closed my eyes. Relief allowed me rest, and I slept better than I had in months.

I snapped awake the next morning at ten. CJ had gone to work at six, but he let me sleep. Bridget, though, should have been up. She went to sleep at nine. She was in her crib; I could see that on the monitor, but something was wrong. I think I knew before I got to her room, before I touched her. I knew when I saw her porcelain face without a smidge of red. Lips, cheeks, nose—like paste. She was cold and firm to the touch. My baby, my Bridget, was dead and had been dead for a while. She might have been dead when CJ checked on her. I knew then that I'd been right the night before. Someone, or something, had taken her. When she came back, she was already gone.

I don't remember calling CJ. I don't know what I said. He says I was sitting in the rocking chair, staring at my dead daughter, when he arrived. CJ called his buddies who came to discretely document the scene and collect my little girl. That was the last time I saw her. I couldn't bear to see, or touch, her again. Not like that. We had her cremated, and neither one of us have set foot in her room again.

CHAPTER 5

BED IS INFINITELY more comfortable than the couch, so I fall into a deep sleep almost immediately. I don't know what time it is, when a loud blast of static wakes me. Once, during a hotel stay, the radio clock alarm went off. It had been set to radio, but not tuned, and the volume set on high. Some childish prank left by the previous guest, but it scared the shit out of me at eight-thirty p.m., and made me slip, while brushing my teeth, leaving a long, sore scrape on my upper gums. The sound startling me awake is just like that, and I look around to get my bearings. It isn't pitch black in our room, although the black-out curtains are drawn. The light comes from the video monitor, which shows Bridget's room lit as it was the night she went missing. The static sound blares from the monitor as well, although the picture is crisp and clear.

I reach over to CJ and try to wake him. I shake his

leg and whisper his name, but he doesn't move. I need to go see, whatever it is, that called me to her room. My heart pounds so heavy in my chest that I fear tiptoeing is a waste of time. I'm not sneaking up on anything. Surely, the whole house can hear the thump-thump of the adrenaline-fueled pump. Although her room sits only about three feet across the hall from ours, the trip feels like the slow traverse across a mine field. Each step forced, yet, suddenly, I'm there. My hand rests on the doorknob. I don't expect it to be warm, but it is. It hasn't been touched in six months, but it's as if someone has been holding onto it. Me? Have I been standing here, grasping it for so long, I have warmed it with my body heat? I have no idea. The night is never ending, and it's been hours since I left our room.

An azure glow envelopes me as I enter. So bright, it takes a moment for my eyes to grow accustomed. I'm almost certain there is not a full moon tonight. Even so, no moon has ever given off this kind of spotlight radiance. Bridget's crib is empty, just as it was the night I lost my mind. No blanket, no binkie. I realize that her blanket never did reappear. I wonder if the crib is warm, like the doorknob. Sweeping my hand across the cotton surface, I find it cold—as cold as Bridget was that morning, when her lips were the same color as the light in the room.

I'm lost. Why was I brought here? Why did the monitor call me to this room? I slowly turn, so that I can take in everything, searching for answers. Then I see them, answers I was not prepared to find. Owls. There are two windows in Bridget's room, one ninety degrees from the crib and one on the opposite wall. Staring into each of the windows are owls. Five total. Three in one window, two in the other. They watch me, as I discover them. They watch as I scream for CJ, and as I scramble from the room, pushing on the door, trying to get out— *had I shut the door behind me when I came in?*—when I should be pulling. I don't look back at them. I escape and run into our bedroom.

Here, it is worse. The curtains are drawn, yet the blue light floods in, filling every empty space. CJ sleeps on the window side of the bed, but I find him awake, or at least with open eyes, staring at the owls, as they stare back at him from our windows, too.

"CJ!" I scream. He doesn't move or blink. I shake him—nothing.

The owls do not blink, either. Their green eyes glow against the cobalt lit room. I can't stay here. I have to get away, I have to hide. CJ can't help me now, so I'm on my own. I grab my phone from the nightstand and leave the bedroom.

The living room's radiance is no different than the bedroom's, so I need to find shelter—one without windows. I don't try to look for more night creatures. Instead, I grab the chef's knife from the block in the kitchen and beeline to the coat closet to cocoon myself within the warmth of empty sleeves.

I find the chat room and enter an emergency request for help. My trembling fingers make a lot of typos explaining the current situation, but my friends decipher it well enough.

RubyJ1976: many alien abductees have seen owls. think they take that form because our brains can process that better?

MIBA51: ur being tracked. If you are somewhere safe and sure they can't see u, u gotta search urself for marks or scars—anything that looks strange, then ur gonna have to dig it out. get rid of it.

RubyJ1976: r u in a safe place?

BridgeMom: M in our coat closet. I ddint knwo where t go they surounded th house i think they mya have got t cj to idk whta to do.

MIBA51: if they wanted to take u, they would have without waking u. u have to find the tracker. get it out of ur house asap. theyr just watching u tonight, keeping tabs. like how scientists tag animals, its the same thing.

BridgeMom: What if th tracker is in cj??? wht do I do then??

RubyJ1976: rule urself out first, honey. thats all u can do right now and stay in there til morning. And keep us posted.

MIBA51: shoulders, neck, thighs, butt—most common places to find them.

I use the flashlight app, and phone camera, to look all over, as much as I can, but find nothing unusual. I can't be sure I've covered all the areas perfectly; it's hard to do alone. I sit back and lean my head against the wall.

I drift in and out of sleep thinking of my baby and Munchausen by Proxy. I can't imagine hitting her with a meat mallet, but I know the pattern our metal one makes in the chicken. I don't remind myself how much I enjoy pounding raw meat with it, over and over. I try not to think about the satisfying squish of flesh giving way to the path of aluminum spikes, as I hammer away. Organized grids of tiny squares, inside a bigger square, layered at various angles until complete chaos leaves a broken and battered, but somehow more pleasing, piece of tissue. I didn't hurt her, but I wonder if they did—the owls from outer-space.

I sit up straight. *Bridget.* I know they took her. I know they brought her back. And I know that autopsies don't look under the skin for trackers. They only look deep inside for reasons. When they don't find any, they say things like "sudden infant death syndrome" and "postpartum psychosis" before they cremate her body and give it back to us in a box. CJ moved her ashes to the urn that sits on the mantle, not me. I couldn't bear it at the time.

What if the tracker is still with her?

The coat closet is, by my estimation, fifteen steps down the hallway, a ninety degree turn to the right, and then an additional ten steps across the room from the fireplace. My concern is the windows that sit on either side of the mantle. If they see me come for the urn, will they realize what I'm about to do? Should I wait until morning like RubyJ1976 suggested, and then look? It's the safest thing to do, for sure. My phone says it is four-fifteen a.m., so it won't be long, but the more I think about her ashes, the more certain I become the tracker is there. Why would it be in CJ? He's never around, and he is strong enough to fight them off.

I'm going to go get Bridget. I belly-crawl through the hallway, keeping to the darkest part of the room. I stop at the couch and slink behind its bulk. It's tight and hot in this space, hard to breathe, and even harder to slide along the faux suede. But if I can do it, I'll come out beneath the window and can continue my crawl toward the mantle. I feel the sofa move, just a smidge, as I wriggle along, but I don't think it is too much to notice. Besides the blue atmosphere of the room, I can't even be sure they're watching; still, I take no chances. The air thins when I reach the side table, and I breathe in a single gulp. It tastes funny, the way electricity smells, but it rushes into my lungs easily, so for that, I'm thankful.

I scrape my shin as I slide beneath the table and window. It hurts and brings tears to my eyes. I want to cry, to bawl like a baby with colic, but I bite my lip. Now I have to stand in order to grab the urn. I don't think I'll be able to retrace my clandestine trip through the furniture while holding her, so I will have to make a run for it instead.

With Bridget in hand, I cross the living room in four graceful leaps and skitter down the hallway like a mouse. Back inside the closet, I accidently cut my hand sweeping in the darkness for the knife. I should have turned the phone light back on, but I didn't want to immediately call attention to my location. I don't think the cut is deep, just more of a fillet of skin on my palm. I feel the warmth of blood filling the space between layers of flesh. This is a problem. I don't want it to mix in with the ashes. I know CJ often keeps rubber gloves in his work coat. After an awkward search in the cramped, dark space, I find one.

If I do this, I will be sacrificing some ash to the floor crevices. I realize I should have brought a cutting board or something in with me, but there was no time for thinking ahead. I turn the flashlight back on and lean the phone against the wall so I have both hands to work. I wipe any traces of myself off the knife onto my pantleg. Knowing in my heart that Bridget would want me to solve this mystery and protect her family, I dump her ashes onto the floor.

Using the knife, I cut lines of ash and then sift through it with my ungloved left hand, feeling for any chunks or pieces of metal. Once I am satisfied, I brush the line onto the blade and carefully dump it back into her urn. I do this until the closet door is suddenly swung open and daylight rushes in to blind me. I scream.

"What the fuck are you doing?" CJ rages.

"I, I, um…" I stammer. How do I explain this rationally?

He grabs my arm hard and yanks me out. The knife clatters to the floor, and my foot accidentally trails through the ashes. CJ grabs the knife—probably his cop instincts telling him to get the weapon away first—as if I would stab him. That's when he sees Bridget's urn and the scattered remains.

"Lena. I cannot even begin to understand what this is all about." His eyes continue to evaluate the scene. I watch them and narrate his thoughts as if they are my own. *What is she doing with one of my gloves on? And why just one hand? How could she dump our daughter out onto the floor of a closet? Is there blood under that glove? Has she hacked up any of the coats? No. They seem fine. There is no blood on this knife, just dust. But what was she doing in there? She's got her phone.* He grabs it, looks at the screen open to my chatroom, and tosses it back to the floor. I hope he didn't break the screen. I want to pick it up and check, but I dare not move.

"Take the glove off." I obey. It sticks a little to the blood on my palm. He grabs my hand and inspects it. "What were you doing with her ashes?"

"You wouldn't believe me anyway, so why ask?" The fact is, in the light of morning, I suddenly feel stupid and foolish. I've dumped my daughter onto a dirty floor and contaminated her remains with who knows what, as well as losing some to the environment. What was I thinking?

"Try me."

"Okay. I was looking for a tracker. Something the aliens embedded in her when they took her. Something that allows them to come back and find us, watch us. I thought, if I found it, I could take it away and throw it into the woods, or something. To keep us safe."

He hangs his head and breathes. The knife is still in his hand, and I wonder if he is thinking that slitting my throat might be the best way to end my madness. Would I try to stop him if he did? I don't know.

Finally, he looks at me again. "I'm calling Dr. Preston and taking the day off. We'll go together. This has to stop, Lena. I don't want to have to put you into an institution."

I stand up and brush Bridget off my legs. "This isn't the 1800's, CJ. You don't get to declare me crazy, and lock me away, so you can go live a free bachelor life."

"Please, just go take a shower and clean yourself up."

CHAPTER 6

WALKING INTO DR. PRESTON'S basement office, with CJ, feels more like walking down death row to the electric chair, rather than Hell. Maybe this time, I will sit on the chair as a sort of joke. I laugh a little to myself so that only a small puff of air escapes my nose. CJ notices and furrows his brow. I shrug.

I go straight to the couch as CJ waits for his tea. He even asked what kind she had. Turns out, she has a lot of options, and CJ says, "whatever has the most caffeine." I am surprised to learn that green tea has the most. I always thought it was the darkest black teas. Funny how you think you know something all your life, and then find out you're wrong. I expect CJ to sit beside me on the couch, but he goes straight to the chair—my chair—plops down, grabs a coaster, and puts his tea on the small side table. I'm shocked at his audacity, but maybe I'm more ashamed of my lack of social skills.

Once Dr. Preston is situated in her chair, with my folder and her tea—definitely black tea with a wedge of lemon floating on top—she looks at me and then at CJ.

"CJ, you called me this morning because Lena had a rough night, and you were clearly worried about her. Can you tell me more about what happened, from your perspective?"

CJ wastes no time in retelling the horrific tale of Lena, hiding in the closet with a knife, digging through his daughter's remains.

Dr. Preston looks at me. "What were you doing, Lena? It sounds, to me, like you were frightened of something."

"What is that sculpture made of? Is it bone?" I point to the bone white twist on her mantle. I'm not trying to stall or avoid the question. It's just that CJ was so bold, with his tea request and chair selection, I feel emboldened. Dr. Preston ponders my question.

"You see what I mean? It's like she is never all there anymore. Her mind drifts, and her excuses are just outlandish." CJ gestures to me with his arm outstretched and palm up—the universal… *I present this monstrosity for your consideration.*

But Dr. Preston puts her hand up without breaking her focus on the sculpture.

"Hmm, I don't know, Lena. I never thought about it. Might be bone or made to look like it. I just loved the turns and curves. It reminded me of what a thought might look like. What does it look like to you?"

"Bone. Of some sort." I shrug because I know, if it was an inner ear bone, then it would belong to a giant, and giants don't exist. I shouldn't have asked. Now, there is more about me to judge. I decide to change the subject back to her original question. "I woke up because the monitor came on, except that the sound was all static." I go on from there. CJ listens without interrupting, and I am thankful. Dr. Preston stirs her tea so often, the sound becomes a metronome. I try to keep my story in rhythm with the *tink, tink, tink* of the spoon. I tell them everything, leaving nothing out.

I finish, and they both stay quiet. Then Dr. Preston asks, "Before having Bridget, did you ever think about, or believe, you were the victim of alien abduction?"

CJ interrupts before I can answer. "Don't encourage this. It's severe postpartum depression worsened by grief and guilt. She is going crazy right in front of me. And, if we don't get this under control, she'll have to be institutionalized for her own good." He leans over and puts a hand on my knee. I don't feel comforted. I feel held down. The pressure is not love; it is control.

I decide to ignore him and answer Dr. Preston. "No, I don't remember ever having thoughts of being abducted or having strange things happen, the way they have since Bridget."

Again, CJ speaks. "She had night terrors as a child which developed into sleep paralysis."

Now it's Dr. Preston's turn to sit up and lean into the conversation. "A lot of people see terrible and frightening things during sleep paralysis."

"That's not true, CJ. I had a lot of nightmares, but I was never diagnosed with sleep terrors or paralysis. If anyone has it, it's you. I tried to wake you last night. I tried to show you what I was seeing, but you didn't move. Then your eyes were open, yet you still wouldn't get up, and you didn't listen to me."

"Do you think you're looking for some way to excuse, or forgive, yourself for Bridget's passing, Lena? Do you feel guilt for that night?" Dr. Preston asks.

"Of course, I feel guilty. I should have gotten up to check on her as soon as I saw she was gone on the monitor. I should have held her when she came back. I shouldn't have fallen back to sleep." I'm crying, and I'm angry, and I feel like there is another me inside that wants to burst out of my skin and scream like a wild animal, before trashing everything in the room. The wild me wants out, wants to claw CJ's eyes out and shove Dr. Preston backwards in that big, stupid, royal chair.

"Bridget. Died. Of. SIDS. No one, *NO ONE* did anything they should feel guilty for. These things happen. They suck, but they happen, and life has to go on. *We* have to go on." CJ is grinding his teeth. I hear it as he tries to talk through them. Is he suddenly on my side? The man is so fickle.

Dr. Preston hands me a box of tissues. I take two rather than the whole box. I should have taken the whole box, but I will make do.

"CJ," Dr. Preston says. "Do you think that you have been as supportive as you could have been throughout this process? Lena has told me that you worked nights

40

during her immediate postpartum, and how she often felt alone and overwhelmed."

I hang my head. I don't want him to know that. I don't want him to be angry, because I'm so weak. I am not the woman he married. That girl was smart, she had ambition, and she laughed all the time. She cared about the way she looked, and she liked to go to the gym with him. But that girl died of SIDS too. I peek up to see Dr. Preston looking at CJ, waiting for a response. CJ rubs his hand on his leg and studies the polka dotted painting.

Dr. Preston might be on my side for real, though. I think she wants me to get better. I decide now is the time to bring up the conference. If I get her blessing, CJ can't say no. I speak up.

"I found a conference—well, a grieving mothers support group I follow online posted about it, so I wasn't looking, exactly. It's about SIDS, postpartum depression, and grief. I thought, maybe, being with other people who've gone through this might help."

"When? I can't just get time off to go with you at the drop of a hat, and you sure as hell can't go alone," CJ yells. He is taking out his frustration with Dr. Preston on me. He wants her to be on his side. He wants her to say I am crazy.

To make the situation worse, Dr. Preston stops his rant. "I received some material about this conference. In fact, I was going to mention it to Lena." She smiles reassuringly at me. "I think it would be good for her, and I don't see why she can't go alone. She is a bright woman. I have no doubts that a trip alone is possible. I actually think it would be quite good for her."

"And I think it's a bad idea with all these violent seizure cases out there. She won't be safe. It's spreading." CJ side-eyes me. I know he doesn't want to talk about this in front of me, because he thinks I will turn it into an alien conspiracy. I should tell him that MIBA51 has already beat me to it.

"I've seen some articles linking them to a newly discovered pork tapeworm. Something like cysticercosis. But from what I understand, there is a paucity of pathologic findings." Dr. Preston seems to know everything about everything.

"That's because these seizures, they happen out of the blue. The person goes wild—biting, kicking, scratching. Then, when the seizure is over, they don't remember anything. They don't realize they acted like that. And it doesn't look like a seizure, so even family members are confused. Many are probably not reporting it, afraid of what might happen to their loved one. It's like a zombie plague, but the zombies are still alive and revert back to themselves. I think this uptick in violent crimes with no apparent motive, these muggings, rapes, and beatings, are all related to this *cyst-circus* disease you're talking about. No one knows."

"I just won't eat any pork," I say. Dr. Preston smiles at me again, and winks.

"I think she should go. I think she'll be okay, because she is an adult woman and perfectly capable of defending herself. Besides, she isn't going clubbing. She's going to be inside, at the conference, most of the time."

"You just don't know who could have it. What if some random stranger sitting beside her at the conference goes all crazy and attacks her?" CJ does not want me to go.

"CJ! You got bit by one! Maybe I'm safer away from you," I counter.

"You were bitten?" Dr. Preston asks. CJ holds up his bandaged wrist. She seems satisfied with this.

"I'm on antibiotics, and I feel fine. I am fine." He sighs. "But I guess if you think this will help her, then she should go."

I'm stunned. I didn't even want to come here today, but now, I'm the winner. I get to go to Amherst and meet with other abductees. Yes, it *will* be good for me, just like Dr. Preston says.

"Lena, shall we make an appointment the week you get back? I'd love to hear about it."

"Sure," I say, and she fills out an appointment card.

CHAPTER 7

CJ IS SILENT on the ride home, but I am okay with that. Silence equals kindness when it comes to my husband. I stay quiet, too, though I am thinking about Dr. Preston. Maybe I judged her too harshly? She does seem to want to help me. I will try to remember more about the time when Bridget was alive. I want to be able to talk to her about everything.

"Want to grab a pizza and some beer? We'll day drink until we're shitfaced," CJ asks. I look at him, trying to determine if this is a trick. He smirks, and I wonder if he is thinking about Dr. Preston, too.

"I would like that, but no banana peppers this time. They smell bad."

He laughs and agrees. We stop at Tipsy-Pies and have a drink while we wait for our order. It feels like old times, before the pregnancy, before we understood what grieving really was. We can never really go back there.

PARTUM

CJ and I carry a hole that was dug out of our souls and filled with a special kind of horror and pain that is reserved for parents who lose a child. Nothing else can fill the hole or soothe the burning ache, so, all I can do is go on and pretend I don't feel it. Ignore it and push it to the back of my mind. But it's there, behind every smile, every laugh, and every sigh of satisfaction, never allowing any other emotion to be complete—even hiding in our love for each other.

Tonight, we're ignoring that pain. And it isn't until we sit down on the couch, with full bellies and dizzy heads, that I decide it's time to acknowledge it.

"CJ, do you remember much about the time Bridget was alive?"

He looks at me and brushes the hair from my eyes. "What kind of question is that, Lena? You know I do. She was my baby, too."

"No, I mean, I know she was, and I know you remember her, but Dr. Preston asked me about how it was. Did I sleep? Did you help? Did we have good days or nights? I can't remember."

"You really want to do this right now, Leen?" He pulls his arm away, and I feel bad, but I need to know.

"I think if I face it, it will help."

He seems to consider this and then nods.

"Okay. I know I was on nights, and I wasn't there as much as I should've been. You were a zombie, but you were a good mom. I remember one night I was home, and she cried. You got up and went into her room, and she immediately quieted down. I don't know how long you stayed with her, but she stayed quiet the rest of the night. When I woke up the next morning, you were back in bed. I asked what you thought was wrong with her the night before. You looked at me and said, 'oh, was she crying?'. I laughed and said, 'uh, yeah, Lena, she was crying really hard, and you went into her room.' And you were like, 'oh, yeah, okay. I did.' That's the kind of responses I got from you. Sometimes, I'd get home and find you lying flat on your back, tears streaming down your face, but sleeping. Sometimes, your eyes were even open, and it kinda freaked me out. But I gotta tell ya, Leen, Bridge was a great baby. She hardly ever cried. She was happy and smiling all the time."

I am shocked. "She cried all the time, CJ. She had colic. I never slept."

"Honey, you did. You slept a lot. During the days, it was almost always Bridge and me. On nights when I was home, she slept great. If she cried, you'd get up and go in, but I'm telling you, she was a great sleeper."

My daughter's cries haunt my dreams. I still wake up at night hearing them. If I held a seashell up to my ear, I wouldn't hear the ocean, I would hear Bridget's screams. They're etched on my ear drums.

I have to go further. "The night she died, when I said she was gone, you checked on her and said she was fine, but you didn't touch her. I remember. That morning, when you got up for work, did you look in on her again? Did you kiss her goodbye?"

CJ sucks in a deep breath. "I never touched her. She was sleeping, and you'd been so upset. I didn't want to wake her up. I should have. I know that now. I should've touched her or kissed her, or something. You shouldn't have been the one to find her like that, alone. You were already so fragile."

That didn't stop you from pressuring me to have sex. I want to say the words to him, but I don't. Instead, I push him further. "When did you smell the ammonia? Was it in the night, when you checked on her, or the morning, afterward? Was it strong?"

"Lena, let's not do this."

"Just tell me, please. I need to know."

"Okay. I smelled it when I went in that night. It was strong, but, I guess maybe, I was too tired to register what it was I was smelling. I was too tired to discuss it with you. That morning, I looked in on her and smelled it again, which reminded me to tell you not to use so much when you cleaned. Then, well, everything went to shit."

"Yeah," I say, because everything did go to shit.

He looks at me and cocks his head to the side, like a dog trying to understand what his master has said. "You went in her room first that night. Didn't you smell it?"

I think about that. I was the first one in the room, and I found her dead the next day—why didn't I notice the smell, if it was so strong? How did I not notice that? I saw the blue light. I saw the monitor change, but I didn't notice the smell.

I'm still thinking when he says, "Hey, I don't want to talk about this. I don't want to think about what happened last night or six months ago. I want you to get better, and that means you have to move on from this. I trust Dr. Preston, and I'm going to trust you to go to this thing, because it's probably the last-ditch effort to save our marriage. I'm going to try my hardest to be better, but you have to, also. I can't live like this much longer. I don't ever want to see our baby's ashes all over the floor and your crazed face looking up at me as if I'm the scary one." CJ breaks down and starts sobbing.

I don't know what to do. I've only seen him cry like this once before, and that was the day we picked up her ashes. He didn't cry when she died, and he didn't cry during the funeral. Maybe he was letting me have my turn. I don't know. But, I remember when we picked up her ashes. We sat in the car, while he sobbed like this, and I stared at the road, willing the car to start on its own and follow my line of sight the whole way home.

I can't pretend catatonic grief right now, though. Instead, I wrap my arms around him, and I hold him. He cries for a while and I shush, shush, shush. I kiss his head. He looks up at me, and we kiss. Suddenly I'm drowning beneath the weight of CJ and his needs. His kisses and tears cover my face and neck. He lifts me up off the couch and carries me to our bedroom.

As he undresses me, I can't help but look at the monitor. It is off and silent. I'm on the bed, and CJ is on me. He thrusts and grunts and nips at my shoulders. He grabs my ass cheek in the palm of his hand and squeezes until I yip in pain. This only encourages him, and he shoves himself deeper inside me. I don't know this man on top of me. I've never been with him like this. I want to push him away and yell, "NO! Stop!" but I don't. He is my husband, and he has needs, just as I do.

The monitor flickers—I think—in my peripheral vision, so I turn my head to watch. I don't blink, I don't take my eyes away, not even when CJ grabs my hair and grinds his hips against mine. I watch for a flicker of static, or the eyes of the owls, as CJ cries out a chain of profanities. I wonder where the tracker is that brings them back, even after Bridget is gone. CJ rolls off me and pants hard to catch his breath. I have to pee, so I stop watching for a moment.

When I return, CJ is snoring, and the baby monitor has nothing to offer.

CHAPTER 8

C J'S SNORES HAVE never bothered me. They are slight and almost comforting, but I can't sleep, so I slip out of the room. I need to check in with the chat group. When I log on, I see tons of messages to me, and about me, that I've missed in the last twenty-four hours. I interrupt a conversation about the agenda for the conference.

> **Dr.BkyVA:** I'm quite interested to see if the historian is going to tie the recent violent attacks to the ancient alien theories.
>
> **AlienAlli:** OMG! @BridgeMom! is that you? what happened?!?!?
>
> **BridgeMom:** im ok. DH found me in closet, no tracker in the ashes. made me go to counselor but she agrees i should go to the postpartum conference.

thanks for the idea.

AlienAlli: we were so worried about you. glad ur ok. yay for coming to the conference!!

TomSmith: Are you still flying in to Boston then? When? What airline?

BridgeMom: was just about to buy tickets. idk yet.

TomSmith: Let me know. The ride share offer still stands.

RubyJ1976: so it sounds like our little chat group will all be going. have you all looked at the lectures/events page?

MIBA51: anyone going to sign up for the hypno regression session?

BridgeMom: i think I'd like to. But idk about doing it in front of an audience

RubyJ1976: an audience of friends, love.

TomSmith: Yes, you are part of our family.

BridgeMom: im interested in the signs of alien abduction lecture. i hope they talk about ammonia and owls.

MIBA51: they will.

AlienAlli: @BridgeMom—go buy ur tickets and let us know when ur getting in. would love to have a couple drinks with u and we can share a room maybe too! 😊

BridgeMom: Ok. will let you all know. can't wait to meet in person next week. im in for room sharing for sure!

AlienAlli: great, I'll let them know and DM you my number. text me when u get in.

I log off and buy my plane ticket. After that, I print up the agenda for the Boston conference, so I can coordinate where I am supposed to be with where I will really be. I leave it lying on the table for CJ to see. I have never lied to him like this, so I have to be careful and think everything through.

Sleep has yet to come for me. I decide a warm bath and a drink might help. The shelf of booze in the garage offers an infinite number of options for cocktails, but it's been so long since I had one, my head spins trying to decide. I grab one with a green label, because lime green is my favorite color, and its hue catches my eye. With a glass of apple brandy on the rocks, I ready the tub.

In the mirror, a tired woman with dark circles and brittle strawberry blonde hair stares back at me. Bones jut out, giving her once smooth, curved body an angular look. Her skin is dry and has the color of an old, but much-loved, book that has been passed around far too many times. I'm looking for insertion sites. Closer and in a better light than the cell phone in the closet offered. I look behind my ears and inside my belly button. I move my hair to see my scalp. Nothing unusual, nothing that doesn't feel like me.

The brandy burns on the way down, and I follow it as long as I can until it becomes a part of my body. I take another swig and try to track it farther this time. When that doesn't work, I give up and slip into the water.

Am I crazy? Would I know if I was? Before Bridget, I was so sure of myself. Confident and independent. It's been almost a year since she was born, so any hormonal irregularities would have worn off by now. I should go to the postpartum depression conference. I should grieve.

I close my eyes and see the blue light. The static of the monitor roars inside my head offering no peace. I finish the apple brandy. The answer is clear through the bottom of the glass—I will go to the alien conference.

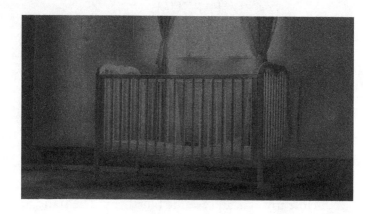

CHAPTER 9

T HE REST OF the week goes on without further midnight visits, and I find sleep more nights than not. Three days before my departure, I stop watching the news. There are far too many cases of violent outbursts that social media calls 'Pork Rage.' The news media and medical community call it Hyde Syndrome or, more accurately, Parasite Induced Aggression. CJ doesn't tell me about local cases anymore, but I know they're on the rise. I see the scratches and torn uniforms. I'm on my best behavior, too. He never finds me in the chatroom, and dinner is always made when he gets home. I smile a lot, and we have sex. He keeps his bite covered, but I've seen the redness blooming around the dressing and the streak of pink working its way up his arm.

CJ kisses me goodbye at the airport, and I board the plane. I've never traveled alone before—I am both anxious and excited. A woman about my age sits beside me and introduces herself.

"You look a little nervous—first time? I'm Jen, by the way."

I offer her a quick smile. "Lena. Not my first time flying, just my first time alone."

"Ah. Business or pleasure?"

"Um…I'm going to a conference, but not for work, just personal education. You?"

"Well, it's certainly not for pleasure." She laughs, but I don't know why it's funny.

She tilts her head back against the seat, sighs, and closes her eyes as the plane takes off. I watch the world fall away out the window.

Once we are in the air, Jen thumbs through a magazine, and I wish I'd brought a book or headphones. She snorts and shows me a "life-sized bigfoot statue" on sale for $3,500. "You in the market for some garden statuary?"

I chuckle and look at her to decline. Her nose is bleeding. "Oh. Your nose," I say and reach for my purse.

"Shit," she says. I hand her a pack of tissues. "Probably the altitude."

"Are you feeling okay?" She doesn't look alright. Her complexion has turned a pasty off-white, and her skin is shiny with sweat.

"Motion sickness." But it sounds like *moden thidniss*, because she is plugging her nose. I decide not to press, but I will keep a close eye on her for the rest of the flight.

When the beverage cart comes around, I opt for a hot tea. Jen asks for ginger ale. We both accept the tiny bag of pretzels, and Jen asks if they are fun-sized or snack-sized. The flight attendant gives her a polite grin, but I see my own concern for Jen reflected in the attendant's eyes.

Jen scarfs her snack and ginger ale. I offer her my pretzels, and she devours them as well. I've only just had a sip of my tea when Jen starts coughing. She grabs the sick bag and vomits. Even through the blue plastic, I can tell there is a lot of blood inside. My caregiving instincts kick in, and I rub her back. The attendant returns and offers a cool washcloth, which I accept for Jen.

"Sorry about that. Ugh," she says when she's through. "And here I was worried about you. I really don't know what's come over me."

"It's okay, no worries." I offer the token Midwest forgiveness statement, take the bag from her, and offer my tea. While she drinks, I twist the bag and signal the attendant. The smell of ammonia wafts up from the bloody vomit, and I break out in goosebumps.

Once we've cleaned Jen up and disposed of the sick bag, I take a good look at her. Her complexion has taken on a grey-blue hue, and her skin looks like thick putty. Her eyes are bloodshot and crimson tears, held back only by osmotic pressure, sparkle in the corners and brim of her lids.

I read once about the Ebola virus and how it causes diffuse hemorrhage. But the smell wafting off Jen is that same odor I've been obsessing about, so I don't know how much of this situation is real observation and how much is just my mind playing tricks on me.

"I wish you'd tell me what's wrong. I have some medical knowledge, I'm a surgical tech." I don't say *I used to be a surgical tech,* because I don't think that will garner any trust.

"I'm fine, really. I can imagine what this looks like, but I'll be fine." Jen reaches out and squeezes my hand, as if she is the one reassuring me. Her palm is clammy and cold.

"Well, I'm sorry to tell you this, but you don't look fine. I'd feel a lot better if you'd let me walk with you, at least to baggage claim, and then see you to your ride, or into a cab, or whatever."

She smiles, a real one that reaches her eyes. "I'd like that, Lena. Thank you."

BY THE TIME WE REACH the baggage claim, Jen is weak. I put an arm around her shoulders to help steady her and keep her from walking like a drunkard. At Carousel A, we wait for our baggage. Jen has one small bag, a galaxy design on the outside. I tell her I will watch for it, and she clutches her stomach and groans. I worry we may have to make a trip to the restroom before we get our bags.

"Just try to hang in there, Jen," I say. "I don't want to leave our bags unattended. Let me just get them first, then we'll head to the bathroom."

She nods, "Mmm-hmm." But neither one of us is sure she can keep the agreement.

Her bag rolls down the ramp and onto the carousel. I wait for it to make the hair pin curve and meet it just on the other side. I set it in front of her.

"Just one more, Jen, then we'll go."

The crowd around the baggage claim thins. Finally, my bag appears. I stay beside Jen until it reaches us before grabbing it off the carousel. I dare not leave her side. When I have my luggage, I turn to see her, slack-jawed and grey.

"Jen, Jen. Are you going to be okay? Should I call for help?" Her eyes are cloudy and unfocused. I'm not sure she hears me.

Jen bends at the hip as if she is about to get something from her bag. Instead, sharp, black, knife-like spikes tear out of her skin and through her clothes as her body continues its forward fall. My new friend splits in two, and a large insect-bat hybrid emerges from the bloody, vertical gash on her back. Instinctually, I reach out to catch her. The creature tears at my arm, near the elbow, before I can snatch my limbs away. I scream and stumble, trying to stay upright.

Others have seen and are screaming too. The baggage area breaks into mass chaos, and security comes running. I am still the closest. I see this thing that has destroyed Jen. It writhes and squalls about the thin carpeted floor. Millions of millipede-like legs, except longer, skitter about, and the spikes on its back have pincers. Longer arms and legs, with a large hairless membrane, spread out as it attempts to right itself among the obstacle course of abandoned suitcases. A tubular proboscis protrudes from its face beneath black, beady eyes on stalks. A tongue, also equipped with pincers, shoots out from the proboscis and grabs at bits of debris on the carpet. I watch, in horror, as it pulls the debris into its mouth. It emits a rubbing, vibrating sound before ejecting a shredded gum wrapper and lost ID tag.

"Get back! Back away!"

I stumble as I retreat, without taking my eyes off the creature. The thing is flailing and screeching louder. I think it might be dying. The clamor of panic, shouts, and screeches overwhelm me. Someone has me by the arm, the good one, the one this thing hasn't compromised.

"Come on, we have to go. Now!" I follow the command, but not before I see the empty shell of my friend, Jen, draped like Dali's clock over her suitcase and hear the gunshot that silences the creature's screeching.

CHAPTER 10

ONCE WE'VE ESCAPED the mayhem of the airport, I look at my rescuer. He is an average man. Average build, average height, sandy-blonde hair cut in the typical casual-businessman style. He is probably late thirties; I see some crow's-feet and frown creases.

"Who are you?" I ask, not knowing what else to say. "I mean, thank you for helping me back there, but, why me? Do you know me?"

"Lena Fitchett, right?" he answers. That is not an answer, though, considering he is not Lena Fitchett. I am Lena Fitchett, and I know who I am.

"Yes."

"It's me, Tom. Tom Smith from the chatroom. Remember I offered a ride share with you? The car was just delivered when I saw the commotion inside. I stepped in among a group of uniformed men. I saw you and realized, whatever had happened, you did not need to be a part of the chaos. I'm sorry if I frightened you."

Tom Smith from the chat group, he says. I realize that I was careless to get into a car with a strange man, and I feel stupid. I know of Tom Smith, but I don't know what he looks like.

"How did you know what I looked like? How did you know it was me?" I ask, realizing that he shouldn't know me either.

He keeps his eyes on the road and does not look at me. "Well, truth be told, I looked you up. I looked up everyone from our chat group. I'm not some crazy conspiracy theorist, and I didn't want to be in a group filled with that kind of people. I investigated all of you."

My mind is everywhere. I keep replaying the scene of my friend being split in two as some demonic creature tore itself out of her body. But, also, I got into a car with a stranger who says he's been stalking me on the internet. *This was a mistake*, I think. *A big mistake.*

He can tell I am nervous and fidgety. "Listen, Lena. I know this all sounds creepy. But I am an IT guy by nature, and I work for a private detective. Looking people up online—it's what I do. I can tell you about everyone in the group."

I'm considering this. I say nothing.

"Alien Alli—real name is Allison McKain. She's thirty-four, has two kids in middle school, and is a biology professor at the University of Nebraska. MIBA51—*Men in Black* Area 51, no doubt—is a retired Marine working as a long-haul trucker. His name's Chuck

Watson, and he's single, age fifty-three. RubyJ1976 is Ruby Jean Johnson; she owns a little café in Ten Mile, Tennessee. She is sixty-three. DrBkyVa is Renee Britton—a forty-five-year-old widowed large animal vet in Harlen, Kentucky. Any questions?"

My head spins with all the information. "What was that thing back at the airport?"

"I didn't get a good look. Probably some asshole smuggling an exotic pet into the country. It got loose and attacked that poor woman."

"That's not what happened, though. The thing came out of her back. It ripped her open. She died. It was like that *monster* was wearing her as a skin suit." I rub my elbow where it got me. I don't know if it bit me or clawed me, or what exactly.

This is the first time he looks at me. It's not the incredulous visage CJ shows when I speak. Instead, he seems to be searching for signs that I am joking or unsure of what I'm saying.

I shake my head, trying to get rid of the image that keeps looping through my memories—black spikes suddenly erupting from Jen's back, followed by her body slumping forward as this creature unzipped her flesh and fell out of her.

"How about some music? Let's not think about what happened back there. When we get to Amherst, I'm sure it will be all over the news, and we can get some answers."

It's fine with me. I'd rather not talk anymore.

"Passenger picks the station," he says.

"Really, whatever you want. Anything but country," I say, which is a lot more than I would usually offer. I'm proud of myself for speaking up, but I know it was in desperation. I simply can't take anymore unpalatable thoughts in my head.

"Huh. Interesting. Country music is such an American cultural staple; I thought everyone enjoyed it."

Now I look at him, assessing for sarcasm, but he seems truly bewildered. "Aren't you an American, as well? You should know we don't all think the same."

He laughs. "You're so right." He tunes the radio to a local pop station.

THE RIDE TO AMHERST IS close to two hours. When we enter town, I text Allison to let her know I will be there soon. She texts back with a room number, instructions for checking in, and information about registering for the conference.

The Briar Patch Inn is a moderately sized bed and breakfast hosting the conference. I read the plaque on the wall and discover there are twenty-five rooms and two large, private conference areas. Our group must be taking up most of their space. This calms me. It helps to know that most people I interact with will not be judging me. Tom leans over and nudges my sore elbow.

"You're up." He nods to the woman waiting at the counter.

"Oh sorry. I guess I zoned out."

Allison is waiting with open arms when I arrive at our room. We hug, and I introduce her to Tom. Tom's room is just down the hall, and he asks if we want to meet up, as a group, tonight at the tavern down the street. I'm tired, but I would love to meet everyone face to face before the conference starts. I give him my cell number and tell him to text me.

"Oh my gosh, BridgeMom, I mean Lena! It's so good to finally meet you." She holds me back at arm's length and takes a long look. "Hon, you don't look so good. You feeling okay? I know lying to your husband is probably bothering you."

"I need to let him know I made it," I mumble. Then, "Something happened at the airport. Something awful and unexplainable."

She sits on the bed—there is only one in the room but it's a queen, and I have no concerns about sharing with her. She pats the mattress beside her, and I sit. I tell her everything. From meeting Jen, to the horrible creature's emergence, to Tom showing up in the nick of time. She asks me to draw this creature. "I'm a biologist, maybe I'll recognize it."

I give her a dubious look. "I don't think so."

"Well, now I want to see it even more."

I do my best to convey the creature's likeness. I'm not artistically inclined, so it looks as though it was drawn by a child's hand, but it's the best I can do. When I hand it to her, Allison furrows her brows and studies it.

"Are these wings?" she asks.

"More like membranes. Like a flying squirrel or if a

bat's wing was attached to its feet. It was a sheet of thin tissue."

"Body hair?"

"No. The rest of it was like a big bug, or caterpillar, with spikey projections."

"Impossible. It can't have a membrane *and* be an insect."

"Then I'm crazy, just like everyone suspects." I'm tired, so very tired. I just need to lie down and take a nap.

"No! Not at all. I don't believe you're crazy. This is all very strange. Frankly, a storm is brewing. I think something major is going to happen soon."

I fall back onto the bed and close my eyes. "I don't want to hope for that, Allison, but if you're right, that's good news for me and my mental health."

"You've had a baby with colic, which contributed to your depression—and then your baby passed away. Meanwhile, all these strange things are happening, yet no one believes you."

"Mmm," I say and fall asleep.

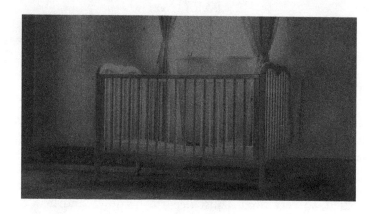

CHAPTER 11

"LENA?" ALLISON SHAKES my leg. I open my eyes. It's dark outside.

"What time is it?" I ask. My stomach answers with a growl, and I try to remember when I last ate.

"It's seven. You want to go meet the others for some drinks and a bite to eat?"

I do, so I get ready, then walk across the street with Allison. We find Tom, Ruby, Chuck, and Renee at a table with two empty seats waiting for us.

I wave, and Tom introduces us to the group. Ruby stands to hug me. "How you doin', honey? We heard you had a rough trip."

I hug back and rest my chin against her shoulder. I did, but I am not ready to talk about the experience. The rest of the table gets up, and we engulf each other in a big group hug. It feels good to be believed and accepted, and I wish I could hug them all back at once.

I eat and listen to everyone chatting about the up-coming conference, the lectures, and get-togethers. I lose track of the conversation as I look around the tavern. The televisions above the bar have just been turned on, and one is tuned to a twenty-four-hour news station. In the baggage claim area of the airport, a police officer is answering reporter's questions. I go to the bar and ask the bartender to turn the segment up. It's loud, though, so I still can't hear everything. They show a picture of a creature called a colugo, before showing an ambulance taking off with its lights flashing.

I am married to a cop. I know that the ambulance doesn't turn on its lights and sirens if the person inside is dead. But I also know that Jen was—*had to be*—dead. No one else was injured, other than me.

Tom steps up beside me and puts his hand on my shoulder. "That thing is creepy looking, but, just like I said—someone was smuggling in an exotic pet, and it got loose. Your friend was taken to the hospital, so I don't think things went as badly as you perceived."

He smiles at me. I think he is hiding something, but I doubt my own mind.

"Maybe I will do the hypno-regression and see how it goes, figure out why my memory thinks otherwise. That thing was not a coligula, or whatever they called it. It was huge and insect-like. I need to know what the hell I saw."

"Lena, can I give you some advice?" He doesn't wait for me to answer. "Don't waste this opportunity over the event that transpired in Boston. There were a lot of other witnesses there. Find out what happened to your daughter—isn't that why you came?"

I don't want to argue. I agree and allow him to steer me to the table, his hand on my back.

The talk has become lively in my absence.

"Well, I will flat out ask them if there's a connection," Chuck says.

"I really think the answer has nothing to do with aliens. It's a newly identified pork tapeworm," says Dr. Britton.

"How do they get tapeworms out of the brain? Is it some kind of surgery?" Ruby asks.

"No, they treat it medically. Meds that kill the parasite."

"What did the news say, Lena?" Allison asks, changing the subject and turning the attention to me.

"It said that the creature Lena saw was actually a coluga. Probably being smuggled in as an exotic pet. It got loose and attacked her friend," Tom answers for me. "I don't think we're doing her any favors by talking about it, either."

It was traumatic, but I want to talk about it. Even more in this company, because I know what I saw was not what the government is saying. Tom works for a private detective; it makes sense that he is looking for logical, and easily explained, answers. But I was there, and I know Jen died when the thing ripped its way out of her.

"A colugo is a small animal. That's not what Lena described to me." Allison is challenging Tom. She doesn't like him, I can tell.

"It was not a colugo. Jen, my friend, is dead. I saw it happen. The thing was inside her. It must have taken up the whole length of her. Its spikes came right out of the middle of her back and tore her open. Then it flopped out, bit me before it fell onto the ground, and tried to crawl around. It was screeching, and it had this long tongue and snout. It was black, like a beetle, and it had millions of little legs like a millipede. Jen fell flat as if she had no bones left inside her. She was nothing but a skin sac."

"Spatchcocked," Ruby says, and I look at her for an explanation. "It's how you tear the spine out of poultry or fish before cooking it, so it will lay flat."

"Yes! That's kind of what happened," I say, more excited because I think someone is listening, and accepting, my story.

"It bit you?" Chuck and Tom say together.

"Yes, I mean, not badly. I'm not even sure it was a bite; it might have just scratched me, or something." I show them the wound. Dr. Britton takes a good look and says I will probably need antibiotics. I tell her I am using some triple antibiotic cream and that it feels fine.

"Lena drew a picture," Allison says and digs it out of her pocket. "Have a look at this, Doc. Have you ever seen anything like this? Could it be some internal parasite for large mammals?"

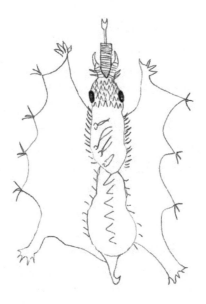

Dr. Britton has a look at my terrible drawing. "Lena, these spikes you've drawn down its back; how many would you say there were? You said the thing was big, like it must have taken up her whole body; did you mean torso, or…." She trails off.

"Her torso, like the length of her spine. It was like each spike pushed through a backbone and tore it out—spatchcocked it." I smile at Ruby.

"Would you say a spike for every bone? Like, thirty-what? Three or four in the human spine?" Dr. B continues to push the question.

"Thirty-three in the human spine, but that includes the sacrum, coccyx, and then the two way up at the base of the skull—the atlas and axis. I know where you're going with this, but where would the thing's head sit?" Allison asks Dr. Britton.

"Maybe twenty to twenty-five. I can't remember, exactly. Jen looked sick the entire flight. She had a nose-bleed, and I saw bloody tears in her eyes, too," I tell them.

Everyone but Tom seems interested. Tom looks frustrated with me, as if I am creating the very group of conspiracy theorists he is trying to avoid.

"So, she was sick to begin with? What if she died of some natural cause that just happened to coincide with this attack?" he asks the general group.

"Or, what if this parasite liquified her innards to eat—you know, like the way a fly predigests—sucked it all up, and then had to go find a new host? We all know the government's gonna spin this to avoid mass panic," Chuck says. I don't think he likes Tom either. I feel bad. It's my fault no one likes him, but I'm here to find out if I am crazy. Tom is like CJ—he likes facts to make sense. He doesn't want to give in to insane ideas.

"I don't know," I say. "Maybe Tom's right. Maybe my brain is so keyed up that my mind is playing tricks on me."

Allison presses her lips into a thin white line, and the others shuffle their feet or fidget with straw papers. My cell phone rings, and I jump. "Sorry," I say. "Gotta take this. It's my hubby."

I leave the table and answer the call.

"Lena! Are you okay?" CJ sounds frantic.

"Uh, yeah. I texted you."

"Yes, then I saw the news. They played a clip from someone's cell phone video, and I saw you in it. Then someone grabs you and pulls you off the screen."

"Oh, yeah. Something happened to the girl I sat next to on the plane. When that thing attacked, I was standing beside her. Somebody grabbed me and pulled me away. I'm fine, really."

"Why didn't you tell me? God, Lena, I knew I shouldn't let you go up there alone."

"Because I'm fine. I figured I would tell you all about it when I got home. I'm sorry, CJ."

"I guess. I just…I think this was a bad idea. You should be home."

"CJ, I need to do this. I do. Please understand."

"I don't fucking understand anything anymore." He growls when he says this, and I can tell he is clenching his jaw.

"Are you okay, hon?" I ask.

I hear more growling and grunting on the other side of the phone, and then a loud clatter before the phone goes silent. I call back three times, but he doesn't pick up. I text, ask if everything is okay, and beg him to please answer me.

I call again and again. Then text. Allison comes over.

"Everything okay?" she asks.

"Yeah," I lie. "The call dropped while we were talking, and now I can't seem to reconnect."

"Ah, bars. The more crowded they get, the worse the cell service. You wanna go back to the Inn? Get a good night's sleep before tomorrow? You might have better reception there, anyway."

I'm exhausted. Even though I slept all afternoon, my body suddenly feels weak. My legs protest standing.

"Yes, I think I'm ready to get out of here."

We say goodnight to the group, and Tom offers to walk us back. Allison declines, telling him to stay and enjoy himself. He does not look like he plans to enjoy anything.

CJ calls me on our walk over.

"Hey, what's with the frantic texts and voicemails? Are you okay?"

"CJ! Are you? I heard growling and grunting noises, and then the phone went dead."

"Uh, shit. I'm sorry. I must have fallen asleep on you. Long day at the office." He chuckles. I've never heard him make those noises while sleeping, but I am too tired to argue anymore.

"As long as you're okay. Thank you for calling back."

"No problem, babe. You oughtta get some sleep, too. Big day tomorrow."

"I'm headed to bed as we speak."

"Good deal. Love you, sleep well."

"Love you, too." I hang up.

"So, all's well. I'm glad," Allison says. "You know, I believe you about your friend Jen. I'm just trying to work out what it all means."

"Thank you for saying that. You're the first person."

"Then it's my duty, this weekend, to add more to that list," she says and puts an arm around my shoulder.

I'm happy to have a friend in my corner, for once.

It feels good, and I sleep deeply for the first time since my baby died.

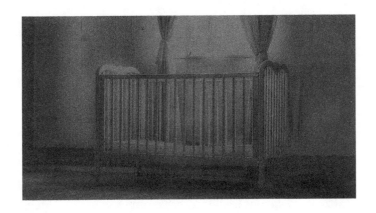

CHAPTER 12

I DREAM ABOUT BRIDGET. I walk to her room, and she is there—sleeping—alive. I'm overjoyed, and I pick her up to snuggle her against my chest. The smell of ammonia coming off her is so strong, it chokes me; I can't breathe. I lay her down in the crib on her back, but she stiffens and rolls passively onto her belly.

Thick, black spears pierce through her sleeper, and she splits open down the center of her back. A caterpillar, or maybe some kind of elongated wasp with a thousand little legs, wriggles out of her. Its body is the size of a ferret, but then it stretches out four longer limbs with skeletal, hand-like appendages. I see wings, which are not really wings, because they are membranous and attached and spread between those longer, more mammal-type, limbs. The creature falls forward, and flops about clumsily, over Bridget's ruined body and all around the mattress.

I step closer to see my baby, but the thing in her crib whips its head around toward me. Out of a long protuberance on its head, a tongue-like thing wriggles toward me. There are pincers at the end of it, and I shrink away, screaming.

"Lena! Are you okay?" Someone is at my side, but at first, I think she is an alien. I hit her and push her away. She holds me tighter, and when I fully awaken, I realize it is Allison. I fall into her embrace and cry. "Hey, hey. It's okay. You're okay. It was just a dream."

I cry until there are no more tears left inside me, and Allison lets me hug her the entire time. When I am finally done, she pushes me back, gently, and wipes the wetness from my face. "Your elbow looks terrible. We better get it cleaned up and wrapped. Then, I think we should get some coffee, and something stupidly sweet, for breakfast before the conference." I nod, because that is exactly what I would like to do.

After we both shower and dress, we head to the bakery just down the block from the inn. Allison drinks her coffee black but orders a chocolate croissant. I choose a caramel macchiato with an asiago bagel, smothered in garden herb cream cheese. She pulls up the lecture schedule on her phone, and we study the document.

PARTUM

SEFK 3rd Annual Conference
Briar Patch Inn, Briar Ballroom
Amherst, Massachusetts - May 15th-17th, 2020

Friday, May 15th

7:00-7:30AM	Registration	
7:30-8:00AM	Welcome	President Anne Comley
8:00-9:45AM	Ancient Aliens	Professor Derek Zyburt
9:45-10:00AM	Break	Refreshments available in hallway
10:00-11:45AM	Modern Evidence	Dr. Mona D'Angelo
11:45-1:30PM	Lunch Break	
1:30-3:15PM	Alien Abduction	Kathy Carlisle
3:15-3:30PM	Break	Refreshments available in hallway
3:30-5:15PM	Interesting Case Studies	Ann Comley

Saturday, May 16th

8:00-9:45AM	Aliens in the Media	Richard Bohnak
9:45-10:00AM	Break	Refreshments available in hallway
10:00-11:45AM	We Come In Peace?	Colonel (Ret.) James McHenry
11:45-1:30PM	Lunch Break	
1:30-3:15PM	Little Green Men vs. Other Non-humanoid Organisms	Professor Janice Strauss
3:15-3:30PM	Break	Refreshments available in hallway
3:30-5:15PM	OWLS	Daniel McCracken

Sunday, May 17th

8:00-9:45AM	Audience Case Studies	Anne Comley, Moderator
9:45-10:00AM	Break	Refreshments available in hallway
10:00-11:45AM	Panel Q&A	All Presenters w/Anne Comley, Moderator
11:45-1:30PM	Lunch Break	
1:30-3:30PM	Hypno-regression	Special Guest, Dr. William S. Asplund
3:30-4:00PM	Wrap Up	Ann Comley

"I think today will be great for you," Allison says, and she is right. I *need* to hear about abductions and any kind of modern evidence.

"Sunday looks good too. I can tell them about Bridget and Jen and hopefully sign up for the hypnosis." I pop the last bite of bagel into my mouth. The coffee and cream cheese has done wonders for calming the adrenaline from my dream.

As the morning ages, the bakery awakens. More patrons arrive and the owner—a lovely, short, gray-haired, grandmotherly woman—turns on the wall-mounted, boxy television to the local news.

"...new study suggests that anti-parasitics have no long-term advantage in treatment of the newly discovered Hyde Syndrome, which appears to be self-limited with symptoms lasting ten to fourteen days."

"That's crazy," Allison says watching the screen. "Parasites don't just die away. That makes no sense." I think about Jen—I wonder if she had seizures for a while, before her parasite grew too big to fit in her brain. I shake the thought away, because that might mean there are more of them out there, and I don't ever want to see something like that again.

"You ready?" she asks. She has seen my response to her incredulousness.

"Sure, the sooner we get there, the better the seat. My mom always said that about church, but I never wanted a good seat there. I wanted to hide, far away, in the back."

"You don't want to hide away today, though, so let's skedaddle."

As we walk across the street toward the inn, I see Tom walking straight for us. He lifts up his hand in greeting.

"Oh good, Lena. I caught you."

I wonder how he knew where to find me in the first place, but I don't ask, because I am more curious about why.

"What's going on?" Allison asks, sounding protective of me.

"Well, I wasn't sure if you'd seen the news this morning, but I wanted to be here for you, if you had."

"What are you talking about?" He steps in with us and continues walking back from where he came.

"Your friend, Jen, from the airport. I'm sorry. She passed away. It was on the news this morning. Apparently, she had a brain tumor and was headed to Boston for some advanced, or specialized, treatment. The attack was just too much for her already weakened body and—"

"No. No. None of that is true," I interrupt. "Jen died in front of me. A monster, Tom. A goddamn alien-looking creature ripped her apart, and I saw it. I know she's dead. I know it because I saw it, and the news and the police, and whoever else, can spin it however they want, but this is all just a load of shit." I look at Allison to see who she believes. "They're trying to cover this up, Alli. It's like you said, parasites don't just die."

"I'm sorry. I didn't mean to upset you, Lena," Tom says.

"Yet, you always manage to do just that, Tom," Allison says. To me, she softens her tone. "Come on, Lena. I need to run up to our room, real quick, before the conference starts."

Allison really doesn't need to go to the room, she says, she just wanted to get away from Tom. So, we get on the elevator and then take the stairs back down, yet still manage to find front row seats for the first lecture. I don't expect much from the talk on ancient aliens, because I've never really bought into all those crazy claims that aliens built the pyramids or taught math to the

Mayans. But two slides in the talk stand out to me, and I frantically take notes.

CHAPTER 13

MODERN EVIDENCE IS exactly what I expect: images of strange looking foreign bodies removed from just beneath the skin of abductees, videos recently declassified by the FBI, and photos of crop circles, scorch marks, and strange bruises. There is no advice on how to find a tracker inside of you or where to look. At lunch, I excuse myself from the group, citing fatigue from a bad night's sleep, and go to the room. I am overwhelmed by the information swirling in my head, and I need to organize my notes.

There was an attempt, by the Aztecs, to hide something in their history. So much so, that they burnt down a large portion of their newly built empire. They practiced trepanning with good success, better than the doctors during the civil war. What were they doing? Maybe just releasing spirits, but maybe they knew about this plague. Maybe they'd caught on to the parasite idea, and they were trying to remove them before the things got so big, they tore out of their human hosts. Ultimately, something similar destroyed their empire. Could the aliens have caught on to what the Aztecs were doing and sent a new, or different, plague for them? The symptoms were like what Jen experienced on the plane.

I look at my notes, which look like the writings of a lunatic. Anyone who read them wouldn't assume I'd stumbled on to some interstellar plan for world takeover—they'd stick me in an asylum. My stomach grumbles and threatens to embarrass me at the next lecture if I don't eat something. I stand to leave when there is a knock at the door.

"Mrs. Fitchett? Mrs. Lena Fitchett? If you're in there, we'd like you to step out and speak to us, for a moment."

I crouch behind the small loveseat I just abandoned. I say nothing. The lamp is the only light in the room but, suddenly, it's a giant spotlight pointed right at me, and the men on the other side of the door have x-ray vision. They can see me. I'm completely exposed. I cover my mouth with my palm and squeeze tightly. I'm shaking and sweating at the same time. The air breaks through my nose in hitches, as if there is some kind of respiratory staircase the oxygen must first climb to arrive in my lungs.

The knocking continues until I hear another voice, a familiar one.

"Can I help you, gentlemen?" Tom asks, louder than needed. He knows I am in here, and he is warning me.

PARTUM

"We're looking for Lena Fitchett. Do you know her?" This is the voice that called out to me. He sounds older, gruffer, probably a lifelong cigarette smoker. I imagine he is broad and tall, maybe six-one or six-two, but mid-fifties, so he's got a paunch, as well.

"Sure. We're good friends. Came to the conference together, in fact. I picked her up at the airport. Can I give her a message for you?"

"Do you know where she might be right now?" This voice is younger, eager. Probably newly hired and driving the older man nuts.

"Hmm, well, the conference is on lunch break, so I'd say one of the many fine eating establishments available in this friendly city. Although, she is also known to be a bargain shopper—always looking at the secondhand shops for some as-of-yet undiscovered treasure. But, like I said, I'd be happy to give her a message for you. Is this about that mess at the airport?"

"What's your name, sir?" the more senior one asks.

"Tom Smith—I didn't see anything. I just picked her up, and she told me what happened. Terrible thing."

"Tom Smith? Really? That the best you can do?" the young pup says.

"That's my name, so I guess it is."

I would giggle out loud, if my hand wasn't clamped over my mouth. I realize this and relax a little. Tom is going to drive them away. Does he really know I'm here, I wonder?

"What did she tell you she saw?" the old smoker asks.

"Not too much, really. She was sitting on the plane

near this lady who was sick, so Lena helped her to baggage claim. When they got there, Lena offered to grab the woman's bags, but when she turned around, something was attacking the lady. That's when I walked in and saw mass chaos and—of course, you know, anymore, you just assume it's a shooter—so I grabbed her and hauled her out to the car." I can almost hear Tom shrug his shoulders. "Either of you two have a card? I can give it to her."

"No thanks. We'll stop back again," the older one says.

I listen to their heavy footsteps fall like rotted fruit on the hallway's thin carpet, until I can't hear them anymore. Tiptoeing to the peephole in the door, I see nothing. No one is there. I stand frozen, still trying to decide what to do. My phone buzzes in my pocket.

<I hope u have your phone on vibrate.> It's from Tom.

<yes. TY for that.> I quickly respond.

<coming down, let me in?>

Less than a minute later, he is rapping his knuckles gently on the door. I open it, just enough to allow his body entrance, before shutting and locking it. He pulls the chain across for good measure.

"Who were they?" I whisper.

"I'm not sure. Not FBI. Maybe CIA? Maybe PIs, but not like any I have ever known."

"What do I do?"

"Avoid them. We are all going to have to work together to keep you from encountering them while you are here."

PARTUM

I'm not sure how to feel about this man. He's keeping something from me, I'm sure of it, but I'm more afraid of the men who want to talk to me than I am of Tom. With Tom, I feel like I know his secret—like he told me once, but I've forgotten, and in a matter of time, I'll remember. It's just enough for me to be cautious with him. But the other two—the smoker and the newbie—they scare me to death. I shiver, and Tom puts his arm around me, giving me a one-armed hug. I don't stop him, but I don't lean into it, either, and he lets go.

"I can't miss the next two lectures," I say, breaking the silence.

"No, you won't. But I want everyone surrounding you, and I don't want you sitting up front. I'll stay back by the entrances and keep an eye out. Maybe I can get Chuck to stand guard, as well."

"They're all at lunch right—"

"No. I messaged them when I messaged you. They should be here any minute. Dinner will be take-out in my room tonight. We can go over a plan for the rest of the conference then."

As if his words conjured them, I hear a key in the lock. Tom jumps up. He peeks out the door before taking off the chain and letting everyone inside. Allison comes directly over and hugs me.

"Here," she says and shoves a Styrofoam clamshell at me. "Left over club and some fries. Scarf it down before we head back to the conference." I oblige. Ruby sits on my other side, and Dr. B sits across from me. Tom and Chuck stand by the door.

I don't feel as if I have the energy to explain everything to them, so Tom takes over, and I am glad. I feel bad about the way we all treated him before, and I can tell Alli does too. Tom seems like the kind of guy to let it roll off his back, though, so long as he is running the show, which, now he is.

"We're going to have to hire you your own personal bodyguard before the weekend's out, you little trouble-maker!" Ruby laughs, and then we all do. She makes me feel better, less frightened and, more importantly, less insane.

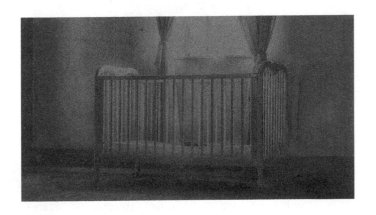

CHAPTER 14

I AM NERVOUS AND cannot stop looking around for two men in suits—one old and one young—coming for me. I listen to the lecturer as best I can, checking off the list of signs of abduction. I am now sure Bridget had been taken more than once. But, also, I wonder if I, too, suffered the same events. Certainly, I've experienced similar issues.

Signs/Symptoms Associated with Alien Abduction

1. Waking up paralyzed, only able to move eyes – *CJ ?*
2. Hearing a deep, vibrating hum
3. Flashing lights or lights with a strange wavelength – *Blue light ??*
4. The smell of ammonia *!!*
5. Missing Time
6. Ringing in ears
7. Seeing or dreaming about owls *!*
8. Scars, marks, bruises – *Bridget*
9. Sleep walking
10. A sense of knowing without an understanding of how you know

During the question-and-answer time, Alli elbows me and whispers that I should ask the SIDS and ammonia levels question. I shake my head. *Not in front of this crowd.* What if those government men are watching? So, instead, Alli stands.

"I have a question. My good friend lost her child to SIDS—" The audience interrupts with the group "awe," and the speaker—a middle-aged woman who could easily be a high school principal in her conservative skirt—closes her eyes, in sympathy, and bows her head.

Alli continues, "The night she died, my friend thought the baby disappeared. She went into the baby's room to check, and the baby wasn't there. My friend was frantic and ran for her husband, who calmly dressed and went into the nursery to find the baby sleeping in the crib. He didn't touch the baby or anything, just told my friend she was seeing things. They fell back asleep, but when my friend awoke the next morning, the baby was dead. She said both she, and her husband, smelled a strong ammonia scent in the baby's room. My friend is convinced the baby was abducted just prior to her death. Have you heard of any similar cases?"

The speaker—Lottie Price—nods, as if, yes, of course she has heard this story before. She goes back to the podium and types into the laptop. We can all see what she types, because it is projected on the screen: **Pattison and Marshall, H. pylori in sudden infant death syndrome.** She finds the article and brings it up on the screen before speaking.

"So, interestingly enough, there have been many

cases of SIDS where the baby's ammonia levels are quite high. This study was done to look to see if babies who die of SIDS are somehow being colonized with the H. Pylori bacteria, which causes gastric ulcers in adults. Through a chemical reaction, the H. Pylori can increase levels of ammonia in the babies, which is thought to have brought about their deaths. The problem is, this theory has been debunked, and no one thinks the babies are being infected. They are still finding elevated ammonia levels during autopsies, but without any explanation as to why. As I said, the smell of ammonia is a commonly noted sensory detail in survivors of alien abductions. Also, the smell of sulfur, lemon, and almonds, but ammonia is the most common."

I know the article she is showing us, because I have a copy printed at home. I paid twenty bucks for access to the study. I tried to get Dr. Preston, and CJ, to read it, but they didn't want to buy into my "madness," I guess. After listening to Lottie Price, I am even more certain Bridget was abducted.

Why her, though?

I don't know.

"Along the lines of this question, I'd like to bring up our next guest to share her experiences. I think your friend would find her story fascinating. I do hope you'll take good notes for her. Sherry DuBries believes she has been abducted many, many times. She calls herself "breed stock" and is certain that she has been impregnated with hybrid babies multiple times. Sherry?" The audience applauds this woman, the one who may have all the answers I've been searching for.

As Sherry speaks, my stomach twists tighter and tighter. I swallow the excess saliva building in my mouth, prepping it for the coming gorge. I can't leave my seat to throw up, though, so I focus on breathing, and swallowing it all back down, as I listen. Sherry says she has been abducted many times for experimentation. She believes she has been impregnated with alien-human embryos and sent back to earth to carry them. She claims when she neared her due date, she would be brought back to the ship. The baby was then removed and kept by the aliens. I think about this. Did they come *back* for Bridget? She was delivered early, at thirty-five weeks, because she wasn't moving. The doctors said her heart was beating strangely on the monitor. I had a cesarean section. Could her early delivery have messed up the aliens' plans? What if they tried to take her, but found she had assimilated too well to Earth's environment to survive on the ship, so they brought her back? Did she die from the shock?

I can't hold back the tears when Sherry is done talking. Alli says we should all leave. She thinks I got the answer I needed, and we should all focus on what to do about the men who want to speak to me. We leave during the break between speakers and go back to Ruby's room this time.

Chuck and Tom decide to walk the inn, looking for the men in government suits while we de-stress. Ruby makes me some tea, and everyone else has coffee. I ask if we can turn on the television, to a national news channel, to see what's being said about Hyde Syndrome.

I see a chart on screen about case numbers and deaths, but before I can figure it out, my cell phone rings. It's CJ.

"Hi," I say nonchalantly.

"Lena, are you okay?"

"Yes, of course. Why?"

"A couple of FBI agents showed up here looking for you. I told them you were at a conference in Boston. Why are they looking for you?

I decide to lie. I don't want to talk to CJ right now. "Yes, they stopped by my room. Since I was sitting beside Jen—the woman attacked at the airport—on the flight, they wanted my take on what I saw, what happened. That's all."

"I should never have let you go up there alone. You should come back right now."

Before I can respond, I hear him flipping out on the other end of the phone. Things break, crash to the floor. He screams and then hits the phone against something until the connection's lost. I end the call. I think CJ is infected.

"Everything fine on the home front?" Allison asks.

"Well, you heard."

"You did the right thing by lying to him," Ruby says. Thankfully, no one mentions the screams at the end of the call.

I glance at the TV, which is now on a commercial for some heart-burn relief. A cartoon version of H. Pylori is stomping around the scene, before a giant pill falls from the sky and squashes him.

"What were they talking about with the graph of cases and deaths?" I ask gesturing to the TV.

"Apparently, people infected with this parasite, and thought to have been cured, are suddenly dropping like flies. The doctors are calling it post-inflammatory ischemic stroke, but it sounds a little fishy to me," Dr. B says.

"Tell her what you were saying at lunch, Doc," Ruby says, and Dr. B gives her a worried look.

"Whatever it is, I need to know. I think CJ is infected. It's even possible I am, too." I rub my elbow, which has swollen even more and has taken on a bright red hue.

"Okay. Well, Allison said this doesn't make any sense. Parasites don't just dig into a host and then die off—that defeats the purpose of being a parasite, after all. There is a reason for humans to be a part of the life cycle. But, I suggested we might be thinking about this all wrong. We're thinking about Earth-bound parasites—basing our assumptions on what we know to be true of things we've studied and have identified. But what if this is an alien-sent plague device?"

"Like in the ancient aliens lecture?" I ask, because this is exactly what I have been thinking.

"Yes!" Allison stands up. "Don't you think it's actually kind of brilliant to introduce a predatory species to eradicate the target species before just dying off itself?"

"Brilliant," Dr. B agrees.

"But they aren't dying off," I say, and I hate that it sounds like I'm whining. "They are growing and eating away everything inside the human host until there is nothing left, then ripping them open." Suddenly, I realize—"*Then* they die. Maybe it's our atmosphere."

"But you're the only one who saw this, Lena." Dr. B says gently. "It's not that I don't believe you, or even that I don't want to believe you, but…well, everyone else seems to have seen something different."

"And if you believe that, I have a bridge I'd like to sell you up in New York," Ruby says. "Why do you think those government boys are looking for Lena? She's the only one they haven't gotten to yet. She poses the greatest threat."

"What if this is it? The invasion? What if they've sent this plague to weaken us or thin the herd enough to take us on?" Alli asks and shivers.

"They tried it with the Aztecs, I think," I say, and the women nod. We are in a dangerous headspace together. We're either uncovering a plot for world domination, or we are developing a collective psychosis, based on a far-fetched conspiracy theory, that we are making up on the spot.

"Why now?" Dr. B asks.

"Why any time? Because we're ruining the earth? Because we're all a bunch of assholes who can't get along to save ourselves or any other species? Because we had our run, and we ruined everything," Allison says.

"Because we have a perfectly good planet going to waste right in front of their eyes. That's it, if you ask me," Ruby says.

"So, what do we do?" I rub my elbow. The motion

is not lost on Dr. B.

"If you've been infected, we need to get the parasite out of you," she says.

"How?" I ask, thinking about the holes in the skulls of Aztecs and Civil War soldiers.

"I don't know, because I don't know where the parasite is. You haven't had any seizures or even headaches, so I don't think it has reached your brain yet."

"But what if it did?" I already know the answer, but I ask her anyway.

"Trepanning. It's the only chance. In fact, it would be great to get one of those suckers in its larval stage."

"Oh, yeah, I forgot to bring my trepanning kit with me. How inconvenient," Allison says.

"They're not that hard to find. Antique shops carry a lot of old medical tools." Dr. B is serious.

"I'm a surgery tech, and you're talking brain surgery, like we could just clear off this coffee table and dabble at my brain with a glass of wine in our hands. No. No way," I tell her.

"There are videos on the internet with instructions on how to do self-trepanning, Lena. People have done it—with power tools, no less! But, if it comes to that, we could leave and go back to my office. I have a surgery room there. You can stay with me until you start showing signs, or until you heal up, and we know you're safe."

"But what about CJ? I can't leave him to just die like…like Jen." I'm trying so hard not to cry.

"Do you think he'd come? Bring him. The more subjects the better. Plus, I have an underground bunker on my farm. We'd have a chance. I mean, if this thing is really happening, we have the jump on it. We should all go."

"I don't think Lena leaving is a bad idea at all," Ruby says. "But, honey, you can't go back home. Those men will find you. You're a threat to their story. They'll find you, and they'll mess with your head."

"I have to go back for CJ. I can't leave him. Also, I need Bridget's ashes. If this is as big as we think it is, then Bridget's death was our red flag. We owe it to her not to leave her behind as well."

"Okay, you go home. You get Bridget and CJ. How will you talk him into going with you?" Allison asks.

I don't know the answer, but I know I have to try to save him.

"Look, Lena, I'm not going to pretend I didn't hear your husband screaming and smashing things on the phone. I did. If we're right about this thing's life cycle, there is a good chance that it is already too large for us to remove. You may be risking everything only to witness another death like Jen's," Dr. B says.

"I know. I know that. I mean, if you're right, you could euthanize him, though, couldn't you? Can you give him a painless death, at least?" I swallow hard against my tears.

"Maybe, but I can't guarantee it will kill the thing inside of him. We may still witness it breaking out of his body. Are you prepared to see that? Can you handle it, hon?"

"If it wasn't Lena's husband, I'd say we need to record it. We need proof that what she saw, and what we think is happening, is actually happening," Allison says.

"I'll bring him. Even if I have to drug him, I'll bring him. Just promise me that if he's too far gone, you'll euthanize him, and you'll never make me watch what happens?" I'm sobbing. I can't help it. This is all happening so fast and, still, deep inside of me, there is doubt. Doubt that what I am saying is all true. Is it just a mental illness, so far gone, that I have brought others into my madness? Guilt swamps me. Lives may be in danger, because my brain chemicals no longer work together as they should.

"What if we get Tom or Chuck to drive her home? They can help her drug him," Ruby suggests.

"No!" Allison and I shout together. "Not Tom, and not Chuck. I can't drag them in, too." I cannot explain why I don't want Tom with me, so Chuck must also be discarded as a choice, if for no other reason than to not have Tom stand out.

"Bottom line—you can't fly. They'll have some sort of surveillance at the airport for you, I'm sure. You'll have to drive," Ruby says, and she is right.

"I think one or two of us should stay here and finish the conference. We'll take good notes, even try to suss out who might be a good person to talk to. Everyone else should head home, gather whatever belongings they need, and then meet back at my place. From there, we can plan a course of action," Dr. B says, and we all agree.

"OF COURSE I'M DRIVING HER home. That's not even a question, at this point," Tom says, when we tell him and Chuck the plan over pizza in his room.

"Tom. No," Ruby interrupts. "We need you to head to Doc's place and get a computer surveillance room set up. Lena will be fine." Ruby pulled this idea from the void. No one had discussed it, but it is the perfect distraction for Tom.

"She can't do this alone. There is no way. Her husband is a cop, remember? You are just going to let her try to deal with him alone?"

"It's okay, Tom. I'll call him and tell him he was right. I shouldn't be here, and I want to come home early. I'll tell him to meet me at the airport—"

"You are not flying! Not with those agents looking for you."

"No. But I can't tell him one of you is driving me home, either." An idea strikes. "I'll rent a car and drive myself. I can drop it off at the airport, and then call CJ."

"Perfect!" Allison says and then, "Are you sure you're up to the drive?"

"I think some quiet time to think will do me good, actually," I say.

"If we don't hear from you, we're going to come looking," Chuck promises.

"Deal. I'll give you my address, but you'll hear from me."

"At least let me drive you to the car rental," Tom pleads, and I agree.

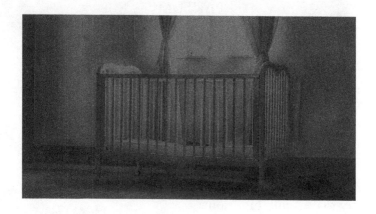

CHAPTER 15

T HE THIRTY MINUTE drive to a car rental company feels so much longer, as Tom lays out his thoughts to me.

"Look, Lena. I was wrong about these people. They are all a bunch of crazy conspiracy theorists. I am not going to Dr. Britton's farm, and I do not think you should, either."

"What?" I look at him, trying to determine what he is thinking. "Why?"

"Because I did some more research on your friend, Jen. Her full name is Jennifer Rose McNally. She did have seizures, and such, before her trip but, Lena, she had a brain tumor. She was going to Boston for an experimental treatment. I have all the local police reports and witness statements in an envelope in the back." I turn around and see the manilla envelope with my name, written across the front, in marker.

"I know what I saw, Tom."

"I know you want to believe that Lena, I do. But every other person, even before those government fools got to them, saw a completely different scenario."

"Really? Are you sure?" This is my worst nightmare—I am insane, and I've somehow managed to bring others into my delusions.

"I'm sure. Honey, do you really think aliens are planning a take-over of the planet? As if all the other planets in the universe are uninhabitable? They want the Earth so badly, they've sent this strange plague versus— and hear me out—all this GMO nonsense, pesticides, hormones, and injections we are putting into our meats. Couldn't those things have caused a strange new pork tapeworm to evolve?"

"But..." I have no retort.

"Have you heard of Occam's Razor?"

I think I have, but I say, "No."

"It says, when given two possible explanations for something, the simplest one is the correct answer. Meaning, at least in this instance, that man has created the abomination, not aliens."

"So, what do you want me to say, Tom? What, exactly, am I supposed to do now?" I am unsure of everything. Even my own decision-making ability.

"Don't go to Dr. Britton's place. Stay home with your husband. He needs you. Recuperate, heal, grieve. Then, when life seems normal again, go back to it. Join it. That is exactly what I am going to do."

We arrive at the rental place. "I'll think about it,

Tom. I promise," I say, as I get out of his car for the last time.

"There are so many wonderous things awaiting you, Lena. Stay home."

I smile at him and thank him for the ride. I wait to see him turn around and head back to the conference, before I go inside.

I DECIDE NOT TO CALL CJ right away and, instead, drive as far as I can before stopping at a hotel in Pennsylvania. I grab some pop from the machine and order Chinese takeout. I spend the rest of the night reading through Tom's research.

I have a lot to consider on the drive home. I am, just as Tom said, the only one who saw a creature erupt from Jen's back. Everyone else saw one jump off the baggage claim and onto my friend. Just like with Bridget, I am the lone man out. I am the outlier. I am the crazy one.

By the time I arrive in Springfield, I have concluded that I am, in fact, mentally ill. I need to see Dr. Preston. I need medication, and, more than anything else, I need to stay at home with CJ, just as Tom suggested.

But I must help CJ, too. I know he is infected. I must stop the parasite from getting so big that it rips out of his body and leaves his empty shell on the ground. I know what I need to do. I may need to do the same thing for me, as well. Bridget would want me to do this. I must...for her.

PARTUM

WHEN I ARRIVE AT THE airport, CJ waits out front with a bouquet of roses and a giant grin on his face. He looks like the man I fell in love with. The anger lines, and disapproving countenance, have softened in my absence.

"Hey there, beautiful! So good to have you home. How was the conference?" He hands me the flowers and kisses me. Close up, I notice two things. First, he is pale and waxy. I've never seen dark bags under his eyes, not even during his worst night shifts. Second, he smells like ammonia.

"Have you been cleaning the house?" I hope for an answer I know I won't receive.

"The flowers aren't enough, huh?" He laughs off my question, and I know what that means.

"They're beautiful and so thoughtful. Thank you. I just thought you looked tired, maybe burning the candle at both ends. I'm worried about you, is all." I fake a reassuring smile.

"Nah. Laid off, actually. Well, put on leave." He sees my luggage and walks away to grab it.

"What?" I follow him. "What do you mean, laid off? Why?"

"I didn't want to worry you, but you know that bite I got? Well, I ended up having a couple of them seizures." I guess my face gives away my thoughts, because he's quick to add, "Don't worry. I did the treatment.

Plus, they're saying now it's self-limiting, anyway."

I knew it. I knew this, and now I am even more sure of what I must do.

"But what about the strokes?" I ask. "I heard about strokes, and stuff."

"I feel great. I think it's probably happening to the people with, like, immune issues, or something. I'm fine, Lena. Can we drop it?"

The image of Jen, in my mind, will never go away. I rub my elbow, where my own bite is red and swollen, with the tell-tale line starting up my arm.

"Let's go home," I say, because I can't think anymore.

It isn't until we get settled in the car that CJ turns to me. "I know you didn't go to the SIDS conference."

As simple as that.

I look at him. He stares ahead at the road, but he doesn't look angry. "If you needed time away from me, we could have done it a lot cheaper. What were you doing all this time?"

"How do you know I didn't go?" I ask, because there is no reason to lie.

"Come on, Leen. I'm a cop. You think after those men showed up, I'm not gonna investigate? You never registered. You never went."

"I went to an alien conference in Amherst."

"Dr. Preston wants to see you. Preferably today."

"I see."

"I'm not mad anymore, Lena. I love you. I want you to be healthy, and I want to help you get over Bridget's death, in whatever way we need to do that. I called Dr. Preston, and she just wants to talk to you about what you learned, or felt, while you were in Massachusetts."

"CJ, I'm tired. It's been a long, exhausting trip. I'd prefer to go home and sleep." I say this, not because I don't want to go talk to Dr. Preston—I do, actually, I have so many thoughts in my head—but because those thoughts are a tornado. I need to calm down, so I can think. Suddenly, everything I planned in the car ride home seems just as crazy as going to Dr. B's. I don't know what the hell to do anymore.

"You have time to nap. Your appointment is at four-thirty; that gives you five hours, at least. Let's get you home, fed, and washed up. I'll even take you to your appointment, if you want."

"I'm fine. I can drive myself, thanks."

There is no more talk on the way home. The air in the car chokes me with its floral-chemical stink. I put the window down a little, and CJ side-eyes me. Other than that, it's as if we are not even together in the same vehicle.

Once home, I lay in bed and try to get my thoughts in some semblance of order. What I know versus what I think.

I know Bridget is dead. I think she may have been a human-alien hybrid, born before they expected, so she wasn't able to live long in our atmosphere.

I know a parasite is being spread, all over the world, through bodily fluids rather than feces, which is the usual method. I think it is an alien parasite, one which gradually grows within the human body. It connects to the spine and eats all the organs until it runs out of food, then it erupts out of the back and dies in our atmosphere.

I know my husband had Hyde Syndrome, was treated, and seems better. I think he only seems better, because his parasite reached maturity. Since it now controls his nervous system, he has no further seizures.

I know I was bitten by a parasite, and I have had sex with my husband since he was bitten. I think I am infected and will start having seizures soon, too.

CJ shakes my arm and wakes me up. "It's three-thirty, hon. Wanna get ready to go?"

I do. I'm ready. I get dressed, say goodbye to CJ, and head to Dr. Preston's.

FOR THE FIRST TIME, I walk down the stairs without concern about where I am going, without the feeling of impending doom. I walk with a purpose.

"Lena," she says and opens the door before I can ring the bell. "Come in. So good to see you." I follow her inside. "Would you like a cup of tea?"

"Do you have Chai?" I ask. She stops and turns, staring at me before a smile flirts at the corners of her lips.

"I do. Cream and sugar?"

"Yes, please."

"I'll put that together for you. Have a seat."

I don't immediately. Instead, I wander over to the shelf where she keeps her antique pieces of medical equipment. I can identify one more of the items now, besides the lobotomy pick—a trepanning drill. There are various other electric machines, as well. I hear the light melody her water heater plays when the right temperature is reached.

"It'll just be another minute or two for your tea. Mine is green—it steeps at a lower temp than chai," she calls out to me. I touch the trepanning drill. A shock runs through my arm and into my temple, where it feels like the ice pick was just jammed into my brain. I feel a little woozy, so I decide to sit down. I choose the comfy chair, because I am here with a purpose. I am here to tell my story without fear.

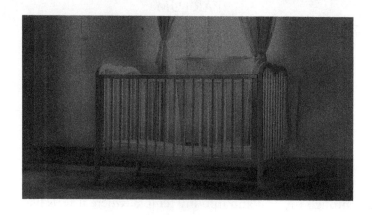

CHAPTER 16

I WAKE UP IN bed with CJ. It is dark outside, and CJ snores beside me. My head hurts, and I can't remember coming home from Dr. Preston's. In fact, the last thing I recall is sitting down in the chair. Did I dream the whole thing? Did I even have an appointment? The trepanning drill sits innocuously on my nightstand. I've somehow taken it from Dr. Preston's, yet remember nothing. I wonder if I hurt her.

The bathroom light doesn't waken CJ. I splash some water on my face and stare deep into the reflection of a woman I barely recognize. That's when I see it. Not through the actual lens of my eye but in the eye of the me in the mirror. Could be a small white thread on my cornea, but I don't feel it, and it moved on its own. Then I see another one. Crawling up my eye and into my brain. For a moment, the world goes dusky, and I begin to lose myself. I grip the cool granite sink until the feeling passes.

PARTUM

I know what I have to do. All those things I thought I knew—I was right, and now I have to act. Without turning on any more lights, I tiptoe out of the room and down to the utility closet where CJ keeps his work belt, gun, and jacket. The snap of the holster is quiet enough, but the damn Velcro closure on the handcuffs sounds like a jet taking off in the quiet of the house. I need him to stay deeply asleep for this to work. I double check that the gun is loaded—it's always loaded—and make sure that, for now, the safety is on. Then to the laundry room where I keep my supplies. This will be the longest night of my life, but, hopefully, if all goes well, it will also be my last.

I set the gun and cuffs on the bin of surgical supplies and tiptoe back into the room. Running the steps through my mind, I decide the first thing to do is get CJ cuffed to the bed. That way, he can't stop me from doing anything else. I will, of course, try to keep him sleeping until I'm ready, but there are just so many preparations that need to be made.

When CJ snores, he is hard to wake. He sleeps on his side, with his right hand tucked under his pillow, bent at the elbow. This one is the nearest to the head of the bed, and I have no problems clipping the cuff on his wrist and weaving it behind the post. The problem is getting the other cuff onto his left arm, which is resting against his waist. It will take some finesse, so I kiss his neck and left shoulder. He subconsciously adjusts himself onto his back, so I have better access. If I continue, he will awaken and expect sexual activity.

Once I have the other cuff on—he is sleeping on his back with both arms over his head—it's time to focus on my preparations, but I take a moment to admire my husband. His chest is exposed to the belly button, and I see the younger man I married. My heart almost bursts with love, pain, grief, and loss. I almost give up, but the end is inevitable. It is inevitable for all of us—I believe this. It's likely just a matter of days.

I have to use his beard trimmer to shave my long hair down to a level where I can use the razor. Once the spot is hairless, I clean it with betadine. I decide to inject the lidocaine before I wake him, so there is no time to negotiate.

"CJ, honey, wake up. Please, I need you to be awake." I shake him.

"Hmm." He tries to roll over, but his hands keep him on his back. He is more awake. "What the hell?"

"CJ, I'm sorry. I had to cuff you to the bed, but I need you to listen to me, and I need you to understand why I have to do what I have to do."

"Lena, what's going on? Uncuff me now."

"I can't. I need you to listen. CJ, you are infected with an alien parasite—"

"Goddammit, Lena. Get these fucking cuffs off me. You've gone insane. It's a fucking pork parasite! I took the medicine, I'm fine. No seizures."

I hate to do this so soon, but I think he needs to calm down. I pick his gun up and point it at him. "Calm down and listen. No more interruptions."

"Lena! Jesus Christ."

I click the safety off and pull the hammer back. He squirms away but quiets down.

"You're infected with an alien parasite. My friends, Allison and Dr. Britton, know this stuff. We figured out its life cycle based on what happened with that woman from the Boston airport." He opens his mouth to interrupt, and I raise the gun again. He stops and listens as I explain the life cycle of the parasite.

"So, right now, inside of me, there is a thing attached to my spine, basically playing puppet master, while eating all my organs? Lena, do you hear yourself? This is insane. How am I still functioning? How am I eating with no stomach? How am I shitting and pissing and fucking, for that matter, without anything inside?"

"Because that's how this works, CJ. The thing is connected to your spine. It controls everything—your brain, your feelings, sensations, pain, discomfort, everything. When it runs out of food, it will rip its way out of your back and leave your dead, empty carcass behind. You have it. You have it, and it is in the puppet master stage. I have it, too, babe. Mine is in the seizure stage. I might have hurt Dr. Preston tonight. I don't know, because I don't remember anything. But I brought this home." I show him the drill.

"What the fuck is that?" I see him twisting his hands, trying to get out of the cuff. He's sweating, but his sweat is tinted red. Blood. He doesn't have long. I have to keep it together. I can't break down now.

"This is how I prove it all to you. I'm going to show you these parasites in my head. I'll show you, then you'll see, and you'll understand."

He shakes his head. "No, Lena. *Why?* What then? You show me these things and then what? I say I believe you, and you uncuff me? Okay, I believe you. Honey, do not drill that into your head. Come on!"

"Then I kill us both," I say. "And we'll be a family again, with Bridget. CJ, you won't survive this parasite. I won't survive it. It's not meant to be survived. They're coming. An invasion is coming. They are going to wipe us all out. They tried it before with the Aztecs, but the Aztecs got smart. Now, they have us. We're dumb. We don't believe in anything. But it's happening. The aliens will take over the Earth. It's a painful way to go, this biological weapon. I don't want us to suffer. So, I am going to prove to you that I am right, and then I'll shoot us both before the pain comes."

He starts to cry and blubber and beg. Snot and spit run down his chin, and I don't like it. So, there is no more talking. I bring the drill up to my temple and begin to crank it. It's hard to do without a mirror, but I need to watch him watch me. I need to keep my eyes on him until I get through the bone. There is no pain associated with the skin, I feel it twist beneath the metal circular blade, but it gives without trouble. I keep turning, pushing harder against my skull. Once the drill hits the bone, both the sound and the pressure are intense.

I keep going, even though it sounds like someone is grinding pebbles against my skull, and my brain is swelling, trying to push out, to escape the noise. I swallow and fake yawn to release the pressure that seems to be building up the more my bone gives in to the drill. It does nothing to help.

The pressure muffles CJ's cries, and for that, I am grateful. My arm is so tired, my biceps burn and threaten to quit. My fingers refuse to feel the handle and ache to be straightened. I push harder and grit my teeth. And then, a loud sucking sound and my head fills with popping candy—fizzing like air bubbles under water—until I am deafened by a loud, wet smacking sound. I imagine my bone is like a boot, long stuck in the mud, finally being freed.

"CJ! I did it!" I say. He looks up to me, his eyes red and his face drooping, coated in a bloody, slobber garland. He doesn't seem to be happy or surprised, or even interested. He looks horrified. I run to the bathroom mirror, fearing perhaps I went too far. The brain has no sensory nerves, after all, and I wouldn't know if I cored out a piece of my own gray matter, would I?

In the mirror, I see what frightened him so much. I look like Carrie at the prom. Blood runs down the side of my head and face. But beyond that, a circular flap of skin dangles from a bright white bone fragment. I've cleaned some tweezers and use them to peel away the osseous manhole cover. The window into my brain is about three centimeters in diameter. I'm looking at the membranes that blanket all my thoughts and memories. I watch it breathe—in and out, in and out—and am mesmerized. But I need to go deeper. I'm sure I don't have much time.

The next step requires a mirror, so I'll stay here and

work alone. I can't think about the blood running out of CJ's nose or eyes, because I'll try to rush and could make a fatal mistake. I must be deliberate for both our sakes.

I grasp the thin, but sturdy, membrane in my tweezers and use the smallest surgical scissors, in my bin, to cut into it and then snip it out using the edge of the bone as a guide. Everything I do is so loud in my head; the echoes of each snip are like screams begging me to stop. But I can't. It's too late. There should be two, even thinner, membranes beneath it, and I try for them next. It takes several attempts, working in the mirror, to grasp the thin sheets called the arachnoid and pia mater, but finally I do and, suddenly, I am staring at my own brain.

Using the extra light from my make-up mirror, I search for the larval form of the alien parasite. They aren't there. There is nothing there but a living, breathing mass of stupid neurons. Stupid, misfiring neurons, defective in every way. I bite my lip and swallow back the tears.

I have to face it. I am insane. None of this is real— not Bridget's abduction, not the owls, not the parasites, not the blue light streaming through my house right now. The clock on my makeup bench says three thirty-three a.m.—the most common time for alien abductions to occur, so I know it's all my mind playing tricks.

"Lena!" The voice shouting my name is not my husband's, but it is familiar, although I cannot place it.

"Lena." That weakened, croaky voice is my husband. Someone else is in the house with us. Ammonia burns my nose and saturates the air.

PARTUM

I walk around the corner, out of our bathroom, and into the master bedroom. CJ looks like Carrie now, streaked in blood erupting from his body.

"Oh, CJ," I sob. It's strange to feel my brain pulsate with my sobs as if it, too, is mourning this situation it has helped me create.

"Lena, back away from him, please." I turn to see Tom. He has the gun and is pointing it at us.

"Tom?" I am confused and step back. He shoots CJ in the head. It's over in a millisecond, but I see it in slow motion. CJ's head extends back, and his body bounces on the bed. Before I can ask Tom why, CJ's body twists in the cuffs, and the black spikes rip through his back and peel my husband away like a banana skin. On the bed, in front of me, is the thing of my nightmares.

Then, it, too, has a hole in its head.

"Tom?" I say again. The blue light in the room is so bright, I squint. I can only see his shadow. I am coughing as I try to breathe in an atmosphere that is no longer benign. He grabs my arm in the same way he did the day he saved me from Jen's killer.

"Come with me," he says, and the blue light becomes everything.

ABOUT THE AUTHOR

EV Knight is the author of the Bram Stoker Award winning novel, *The Fourth Whore*, which won the 2020 Superior Achievement in a Debut Novel category.

evknightauthor.com/

twitter.com/EVKnightAuthor/

facebook.com/EVKnightAuthor/

ABOUT THE PUBLISHER

Sinister Smile Press is dedicated to the publication of anthologies and mainstream novels, focusing on the genres of horror, suspense, thrillers, action and adventure, science fiction, fantasy, mystery, and dystopian. Creating nightmares is our business...and business is good!

SinisterSmilepress.com

Sinister Smile Press

Publisher of fine
Anthologies and Novels

Creating Nightmares is our Business...
and business is *good*!

CPSIA information can be obtained
at www.ICGtesting.com
Printed in the USA
LVHW040017280921
698843LV00002B/96